The Hawk Bandits
of Tarkoom

by Tony Abbott

Illustrated by Tim Jessell

A
LITTLE APPLE
PAPERBACK

SCHOLASTIC INC.
New York Toronto London Auckland Sydney
Mexico City New Delhi Hong Kong

ISBN 0-439-20785-1

Text copyright © 2001 by Robert T. Abbott
All rights reserved. Published by Scholastic Inc.

SCHOLASTIC, APPLE PAPERBACKS, and associated logos
are trademarks and/or registered trademarks of Scholastic Inc.

12 11 10 9 8 7 6 5   1 2 3 4 5 6/0

Printed in the U.S.A.   40
First Scholastic printing, February 2001

For my brother Rick,
who knows that the adventure
doesn't have to end

Contents

One

One Head Is Better Than Two

Eric Hinkle and his friend Julie carefully pulled open a small door under the stairs in his basement.

Errr-errrk! The door's old hinges squeaked.

Behind the door was a small, dark closet, with a single unlit lightbulb hanging from the ceiling.

"Isn't it weird how it looks just like a regular closet?" asked Julie.

Eric grinned. "It *is* a regular closet. To everyone else."

But to Eric, Julie, and their friend Neal, it was more than just a closet. It was the entrance to another world.

The magical world of Droon.

Actually, it was Julie who had first discovered the entrance to Droon.

She'd just gone into the closet, when suddenly the door closed behind her, the light went out, and — *whoosh!* — a long, shimmering staircase appeared where the floor had been.

The kids were scared, of course.

But the staircase looked so beautiful they just had to see what was at the bottom.

On their first visit to Droon, they met a young princess named Keeah who was now one of their best friends.

They'd also met a good wizard named

Galen Longbeard and his spider troll helper, Max.

Galen was teaching Keeah to be a wizard, too.

Together with Keeah and Galen, the kids had battled a wicked sorcerer named Lord Sparr, a strange witch called Demither, and lots of other nasty creatures who were always trying to take over Droon.

The best part was that Eric and his friends seemed to be helping Keeah keep Droon free.

"I asked you over," Eric said to Julie, "because I think we need to keep the closet in good working condition. After all, it's our only way into Droon."

"Great idea," said Julie. "If the door squeaks too much, your parents will hear us. And Galen told us always to keep Droon a secret."

"I'll put in a fresh lightbulb," said Eric.

"You can oil the hinges. I asked Neal to come and sweep up, but he's late."

"As usual!" Julie said with a laugh.

She took an oilcan from the workbench. Standing on her toes, she began oiling the door's hinges. Eric searched the nearby cabinets for a new lightbulb to replace the old one.

As they worked, Eric recalled their latest visits to Droon. He and his friends had had many adventures. But they'd also uncovered many mysteries.

For one thing, Keeah said she remembered being in the Upper World — Eric's world — a long time ago.

But that didn't seem possible.

Then, Keeah was told that Witch Demither secretly gave her some powers. Witch powers!

Keeah didn't remember that at all.

"Hey, Eric," said Julie, bending down to

oil the lower hinges, "what do you think witch powers are like?"

"I was just thinking about that!" said Eric.

"I mean, are they dark and dangerous like Lord Sparr's?" she asked. "Or more like the sort of natural wizard things Galen can do?"

"I don't know." Eric found a new light-bulb and took it to the closet. "But wouldn't it be weird if there was a connection be-tween Keeah being here and having witch powers? I wonder if Galen knows."

"Galen's five hundred and forty-two years old!" said Julie. "If he doesn't know, who does?"

Eric shrugged. "Maybe we will. If we ever get to Droon again."

He glanced at a soccer ball sitting on the workbench. After their first visit to Droon, Keeah had put a spell on it. When the ball floated in the air, it meant the staircase would be open for them.

"I can't wait to go —" Eric began.

Just then, four furry white paws trotted past the window. They were followed by two beat-up sneakers.

"Get back here!" cried a familiar voice.

"Woof!" came the response.

"It's Neal," said Eric.

"And Snorky," added Julie. Then she laughed. "Looks like Neal's having trouble with him . . . again."

"We'd better help him out!" said Eric. The two kids dropped everything and rushed up the basement stairs, through the kitchen, and out to the backyard.

When they got there, Neal was on all fours, nose to nose with Snorky, trying to grab him.

Julie giggled. "It looks like you're dancing!"

"It's not funny," Neal groaned as Snorky romped away to sniff a tree. "I was teaching him to fetch when he escaped!"

Eric tried to trap Snorky from behind. "What was he fetching?"

"A box of cookies," Neal said.

Julie shook her head. "Only *you* would think of teaching a dog to fetch food for you."

Neal grinned. "What can I say? I'm a genius."

"Hey, genius, your dog just ran into my house!" said Eric. He jumped up the steps and into the kitchen.

Inside, Snorky skittered under the table and headed down the hall at top speed, tracking dirty paw prints the whole way.

"Not the living room!" said Eric. "My mom just vacuumed!"

"We'll trap him in the hall," Neal shouted, dashing through the kitchen.

Eric and Julie tore around the other way. But Eric slipped on the carpet, slid across the floor, and crashed down — *ka-thunk!* — taking Julie and a large house-plant with him.

The plant spilled dirt all over the carpet.

"Woof! Woof!" barked Snorky as he turned and shot down the stairs to the basement.

"Oh, no!" said Eric, scrambling to his feet. "What if Snorky gets into the closet?"

"Let's get down there right away!" said Julie.

But when they entered the basement, they stopped short.

Julie gasped softly. "Oh, my gosh!"

The soccer ball was floating in the air over the workbench.

"Keeah needs us in Droon," said Eric. "That means the stairs will be open for us."

"And for Snorky —" said Neal. "Uh-oh!"

The three friends spun around to see Snorky's curly tail disappear behind the closet door.

Click. The door closed softly.

"Yikes!" cried Neal. "He's going to Droon!"

"But he can't unless the light is out," said Eric.

He pulled open the door. The light *was* out.

"Oh, man! I didn't put the new bulb in!"

Below them, the stairs were shimmering in a rainbow of colors. And Snorky was prancing down them, his tail wagging happily.

"Come back here, you," said Julie.

The three friends dashed down the stairs, but Snorky began to run. *"Woof! Woof!"* he barked.

"He thinks it's a game!" moaned Neal.

As they descended through the clouds, the sky over Droon was turning from black to purple.

"It's just before morning," said Julie. "It should be getting light soon."

They jumped off the bottom of the staircase and looked around. Dusty brown mountains surrounded them on every side.

"It looks like the Panjibarrh hills," said Eric. "We've been here before. . . ."

"Never mind that," said Neal, scanning the rocky ground. "Where's Snorky? Snorky! Get back here. You need to go home —"

Then the staircase faded. The kids knew it would not reappear until it was time to go home.

"Too late to send Snorky back," said Julie.

Grrrr. Something was growling from behind a rock.

"Snorky?" said Eric cautiously. "Is that you?"

Grrrr! The growling was louder this time.

"Here, puppy," said Neal softly. "Here —"

A head peered from behind the rock.

But it wasn't Snorky's head.

It was large and gray. Its features were craggy and its skin was rough, as if it were very old.

Grrrr! Another head, the same as the first, jerked up from behind the rock.

"There are two of them!" said Eric, backing up. "Oh, man, we are cooked!"

The first head moved out from behind the rock and the second one moved with it. That's when they saw that both heads were on the same neck!

"That's definitely *not* Snorky," said Neal.

The beast growled, opening both sets of jaws. Four rows of huge fangs dripped a thick, yellow liquid.

Julie stepped back. "That is so — ewww!"

"Don't make it mad," Eric whispered.

GRR-RRR! The twin heads roared again.

"Too late for that," mumbled Neal.

The creature stomped toward them, then stood for a moment, roaring and growling.

Then it leaped at them.

Two

What the Legend Says

"Get down!" Eric cried, grabbing Julie and Neal. The three friends dove behind a large boulder just as the beast pounced.

Thoom! It shook the ground when it landed. Then it turned quickly.

"It's coming at us again!" said Julie.

Suddenly — *hrrrr!* — a six-legged, shaggy animal called a pilka thundered into the clearing.

"Stay back, you hideous thing!" cried a voice.

The kids looked up. Princess Keeah sat atop the pilka, her gold crown blazing in the dim light. She charged over the rocks at the beast.

"Keeah, watch out!" Eric shouted.

But Keeah rode forward, staring down the beast, her eyes blazing. "Begone!" she cried. "Or I'll . . . I'll . . . oh!"

Her left hand suddenly glowed with a sizzling red light. An instant later, a blast of red sparks knocked the two-headed creature back.

Eeeoow! Both heads howled angrily at her. Then, shrinking back, the beast clambered away through the rocks. In a moment, it was gone.

Just then, the great orange sun flickered over the mountaintops, and the purple sky brightened to pink. Morning had come to Droon.

"Wow, Keeah, that was awesome!" said Neal, jumping out from behind the boulder. "It was like that thing actually *obeyed* you!"

The princess slid down from the saddle and hugged her friends tightly. "I'm not sure why it did. But I'm glad it did! Are you all right?"

Eric breathed out in relief. "I think so. But in another second we would have been two-headed-dog food!"

"*Woof?*"

"Snorky!" Neal cried, whirling on his heels.

Trembling, the small dog stumbled toward the friends and leaped into Julie's arms.

"Poor Snorky," she said. "He's shaking."

"He's *my* pet, you know!" Neal grumbled. "I'm starting to think he doesn't really like me."

Keeah smiled. "Come on, everyone. I called you here because yesterday an earthquake rocked the Panjibarrh hills. King Batamogi found something strange and wants us to see. Galen's caravan is just ahead. Let's go meet him. We need to tell him about this beast!"

As the sun climbed over Panjibarrh's famous dust hills, the four friends rode Keeah's pilka down to the valley below.

Before long, they spotted two figures traveling across the plains.

"There's Galen!" said Julie. "And Max, too!"

Galen, his long white beard flowing above a blue cloak stitched all over with stars and moons, rode the head pilka. A tall cone-shaped wizard hat sat on his head.

Behind him rode Max, his spider troll helper. Max had eight furry legs, a pug nose, and wild orange hair. Two other pilkas were laden with supplies and saddlebags bulging with books.

"Hail, friends from the Upper World!" said Galen as the children rode up. "What news?"

"A two-headed beast attacked us!" said Eric.

Galen frowned. "Two-headed, you say?"

"And both heads were pretty ugly," said Neal.

The wizard stroked his beard as the children took turns describing the beast.

"It seemed old, yet it moved very quickly," said Keeah. "Luckily, I stopped it."

"Its four eyes were red and scary," Julie said.

"Also, it had fangs the size of bananas," said Eric. "Have you ever heard of such a thing?"

The wizard looked out over the hills. "I have," he said. "But what you say fills me with fear."

"Why?" asked Julie.

"Because," said Galen, "the beast you describe died four hundred years ago! Now, follow me. Quickly!"

With that, Galen snapped the reins of his pilka and tore ahead. The children stared at one another for a moment, then followed Galen into the hills. They didn't stop until they came to the place where a quake had split the ground wide open.

"So!" said Galen, staring at the jagged crack. "As I feared, this was no normal earthquake."

"Over here, my friends!" called a voice.

A furry creature with a whiskery snout and long, foxlike ears waved from atop a rock. He wore a green crown and a short green cape.

It was Batamogi, one of the ten kings who ruled the Oobja people of Panjibarrh. He jumped down from the rock and bowed first to Galen and Princess Keeah, then to Eric and his friends.

"A big rumbly-rumble shook the hills yesterday," Batamogi told them. "It sent me flying out of bed. I've been shaking ever since! This morning I found it. I called you here right away."

"Found *it*?" said Eric. "What did you find?"

Batamogi pointed to the deep gash in the earth. "An ancient tomb. See for yourselves!"

Galen dismounted his pilka and strode

over to the split in the ground. The wizard was very old, but he moved nimbly over the rocks and down into the ruined tomb.

At the bottom was a small square of earth. Pressed into the earth was the outline of a beast.

A beast that was not there.

A beast with two heads.

"Holy cow!" Julie gasped. "This must be the grave of the great-great-grandfather of that monster we saw."

"No, it *was* the monster you saw," said Galen, his eyes fixed on the outline. "This earthquake was no accident. It was ancient magic that opened the beast's tomb and set it free."

Keeah turned to Galen. "I thought it died a long time ago. Do you mean it didn't really die?"

The wizard did not answer. Instead, he

inspected every inch of the tomb. Finally, he climbed out and dusted his hands.

"The beast is called Kem," Galen said. "It was created by a magic as old as Droon itself. Long ago I fought the beast and buried it here, thinking it was dead. I was wrong, fooled by the dark magic. In his prime, Kem was watchdog of the old city of Tarkoom. He howled like a ghost before attacking intruders."

Eric and Neal shivered at the same time.

"Tarkoom?" squeaked Max. "That was a place of thieves! And robbers!"

"And terrible bandits!" said Batamogi, scratching his ears nervously. "But Tarkoom was destroyed ages ago. You can still see the ruins."

Galen pulled a thick scroll from his saddlebag. "True," he said solemnly. "I was there the night it fell. A great fire reduced the city to rubble."

"Good!" said Julie. "Serves it right."

Galen unrolled the scroll and read it. "Ah, but here lies the problem. A legend says that centuries may pass, but if ever Kem should howl again, Tarkoom would rise from its ashes."

"The city would just come back?" asked Neal.

Galen nodded. "And all the terrible creatures who lived there. Droon's old magic is powerful."

Keeah took a breath, looked at her friends, then back at Galen. "So, what do we do now?"

"We wait in the hills above the Panjibarrh Valley," said the wizard, rolling up his scroll again. "If Tarkoom does rise again, we'll have a most important job ahead of us. Until then, we wait and watch."

Eric frowned. "What exactly will we see?"

"The past," said Galen. "We will see the dark past of Droon coming back!"

Three

Tarkoom . . . Again!

For the next hour, Batamogi led the small troop up one dusty path and down another. They were heading for the highest point in all the Panjibarrh hills.

"Who lived in Tarkoom?" Julie asked.

"Hawk bandits, they were called," Galen said, fixing his eyes on the road ahead. "Half human, half bird. As terrifying to see as they were ruthless. But worst of all was their leader, Ving."

Batamogi nodded, shivering. "The stories say he possessed a strange, soothing voice. It made his victims feel safe. Then he swooped down on heavy wings — *fwit! fwit!* — and robbed them of everything! Oh, Ving and his bandits were feared across all of Droon."

"Until my master stopped them!" said Max, beaming proudly.

"Four hundred years ago," said Galen, his pale cheeks blushing. "But now we must do it again. You see, Tarkoom was a city in the ancient empire of Goll, an evil realm of dark magic from Droon's earliest times. After a long struggle, Goll — like Tarkoom itself — was destroyed."

"But its magic still lives!" Max added.

Galen nodded. "Indeed it does. If Ving and his bandits come to life and work their evil on present-day Droon, I fear the whole dark past of Goll may live again. If I am right, we must stop Ving from changing our world in any way —"

The earth trembled suddenly.

"Another rumbly-rumble!" said Batamogi as Snorky jumped into his arms.

Galen stopped his pilka on a ridge and looked down. "And here we are!"

Below them lay the vast Panjibarrh Valley.

In it were piles of rock, crumbled stones, broken columns, sunken streets, and collapsed buildings.

"Tarkoom," said Batamogi under his breath.

"That's the place?" said Neal, looking down at the ruined city. "Doesn't look too lively."

The earth trembled beneath their feet again.

"Just wait . . ." the wizard said. "Even

now, Tarkoom prepares to return. Let us make camp."

The eight adventurers made a small encampment in a clearing overlooking the ruined city.

Galen sat on a boulder with his scroll and took up the watch.

Max watered the pilkas, while Keeah unpacked some snacks and passed them out.

"Food, anyone?" she asked.

"*Woof!*" barked Snorky.

"It figures!" said Neal, shaking his head. "'Food' is the only word he understands."

"Oh, is that so?" said Batamogi, turning to Snorky and scruffing him. "Well, let's just see!"

The Oobja king let Snorky sniff the cuff of his sleeve. "Now, Snorky, stay here. . . ."

Batamogi backed up slowly, then scurried off behind some big boulders. A moment later, he called out, "Snorky . . . fetch!"

In a flash, Snorky bounded up and, sniffing along the ground, trotted away into the rocks.

A moment later Batamogi waddled back to the camp with Snorky nipping at his heels. "Ho-ho!"

"That was awesome!" said Neal. "Snorky, now me!" He went and hid himself among the rocks. "Snorky . . . fetch!"

The dog went over to Max, curled up, yawned, and fell asleep. Then he began to snore.

"Poor Neal!" said Keeah when Neal returned glumly. "I'm sure Snorky likes you very much, in his own way."

Hours went by. The day wore on into evening. And still Galen read the scroll, kept watch, and said nothing.

"It's getting cool," said Keeah. "I wish we had . . ." All of a sudden — *fwoosh!* — a small fire appeared before them, its flames crackling. The princess jumped back.

"Where did that come from?" she said.

For the first time in hours, Galen moved, looking over at the princess. "You did that, Keeah," he said. "It is one of your *other* powers."

Eric shot a look at Julie. They both remembered what they had spoken about earlier that day. That Keeah had . . . *witch* powers.

"We may never know how you got these powers," said Galen, "but you must learn to control them."

Keeah frowned. "I'm sorry. They seem to come from nowhere and just . . . happen."

"Like when you helped your mother

change from a tiger to a dolphin?" asked Julie, remembering their last adventure in Droon.

"Or when you scared Kem away," said Neal.

Keeah nodded. "It frightens me a little. Well, a lot. The magic seems very strong. And wild. I'm afraid I might hurt someone."

"Pah! Never!" said Max firmly. "You are a very fine young wizard. And I don't believe you were ever alone with any witches. Besides, your father says it's impossible —"

"That mystery must wait, Keeah," Galen said, standing quickly. "Tarkoom . . . begins to wake!"

As the last streaks of sunlight cut across the ruined stones, the valley rumbled even more.

Once. Twice. A third time.

The piles of old rubble and broken stones shivered and shook and rocked and rattled.

Finally — *ka-phooom!* — the ground quaked from one end of the valley to the other.

And it happened.

The toppled stones of the wrecked city of Tarkoom seemed to fly up one by one and set themselves neatly back into place.

Columns, walls, towers, gardens!

Stone by stone, Tarkoom was rebuilding itself from its own ruins!

"Oh, my gosh," Julie exclaimed. "It's coming back. Tarkoom is coming back!"

Four

City of Bandits

As they all watched, the centuries-old city of Tarkoom shuddered slowly into the present.

Where rocks had lain scattered on the plain, now great buildings stood.

Dusty piles of tumbled stones were now the sturdy towers and turrets of a monumental city.

Tarkoom was back, glowing within high walls of red- and honey-colored stone.

And at its center stood a giant domed palace.

"It's beautiful," said Keeah under her breath.

"Beautiful, perhaps," said Galen. "But full of bandits who will try to stop us from doing what we must do."

"So," said Neal, "*their* mission will be to stop *our* mission. But what exactly *is* our mission?"

The wizard let a smile crease his lips as he tapped his scroll. "My friends, we must do nothing less than destroy Tarkoom!"

"The whole city?" asked Eric. "But how?"

"We must somehow use Ving's own plan against him," the wizard replied. "The legend is most specific about this. If I am right, he will mount an attack tonight. If he succeeds, he will have altered Droon in our time. He and his bandits will have become part of it."

"Oh, dear!" said Batamogi. "An attack! I hope not on my poor people!"

"But we'll stop him," said Keeah firmly.

"Only if we hurry!" said Galen.

Leaving their pilkas at the camp, the band of eight travelers climbed down into the valley.

For most of the way, the only sound was their own careful plodding through mountain passes. And the sound of Snorky whimpering.

At last, the narrow way opened up to an awesome sight. Galen held up his hand.

"The entrance to Tarkoom!" he declared.

Hewn from the face of a cliff was a large arched opening. It soared up from the ground as high as two houses. Its sides were cut into the red stone and glowed crimson in the moonlight.

"Awesome," said Eric. "But scary. Look."

Above the opening, a giant hawk head was carved into the cliff wall.

Its eyes were shimmering jewels that seemed to stare down on anyone who might enter.

"That is the image of Ving, leader of the bandits," said Galen. "He loves only himself."

"No kidding," Neal mumbled. "It's like having a picture of yourself on your front door!"

"Let us enter," said Galen softly.

The moment he set foot through the arch — *eeoow!* — the howling of the two-headed beast rose up from deep within the city streets.

"Kem is doing his job," Keeah said with a shiver. "He really is the city's watchdog."

"Which means the bandits will soon know we're here," said Julie. "Be careful, everyone."

They passed into a street lined by columns of polished red stone. The buildings on either side were carved deep into the valley cliffs.

The black holes of their doors and windows were like eerie eyes staring out of the past.

"Everything looks so new," said Keeah. "It almost feels as if we're going back in time."

Galen shook his head. "No, Tarkoom has invaded the present. At this very moment, Ving sits in his palace, hatching his terrible plot to stay in our world."

"And staying in our world," said Batamogi, "means the dark past of Droon will come again!"

"That's why we need to destroy the city!" Max chirped. "So the past will leave the present and go back to the past so our present will be safe for the future!"

Neal blinked. "Will there be a quiz on this? Because I'm getting a major headache."

Eric tried to laugh, but he couldn't. He didn't quite understand it, either.

He paused to sort it out in his head.

"Okay," he mumbled, counting on his fingers. "One, Tarkoom is a city from the past, right? But, two, the earthquake sort of released it from the past, and now, three, it's in the present. Okay, it's some magic thing that only happens in Droon. Now we need to — four — find out what Ving is up to and — five — stop him. Then, six, we wreck the city so it goes back to the past where it belongs. Neal, is that right? Does that make sense to you? Neal?"

Eric looked up from his hands. He was alone.

The others had turned a corner and were already heading toward the palace.

"Hey, guys, wait up!" Eric called out. "Guys!"

Thump.

He stopped. He suddenly felt icy cold.

To his right, he glimpsed something in one of those open windows. Red eyes — four of them — flashing in the darkness.

"K-K-Kem?" Eric whispered. "Oh, no. It's Two-head! It's him! It's it! It's . . . oh, help!"

Eric tore off down the street, but some-how — *thump! thump!* — Kem leaped down in front of him, both heads growling.

Then it reared up and jumped at him.

Eric shot around the corner, but his friends weren't there. He must have taken a wrong turn!

Eeoow! Kem howled and thomped even faster after him. Eric dashed around another corner.

Suddenly, he found himself inside a walled garden. It was thick with hanging plants and vines creeping up the walls.

Kem bounded right in after him.

Eric tried to scream, but no sound came out.

Kem slowed, growling under its breath. Step by step it came closer.

Eric looked around. There were hard-shelled fruits about the size of softballs growing on the vines. He tugged one off and threw it at Kem.

Crack! The fruit clattered and broke on the ground. *Plooff!* It gave off a horrible stink.

"Oh, phew!" Eric gasped, staggering back.

The fruit smelled like something rotten. Worse than garbage. *Worse* than worse than garbage!

But Kem kept coming, closer and closer.

With his last ounce of strength, Eric clutched the hanging vines and pulled himself up the wall, tossing more stinky fruits the whole way.

Crack-crack! Plooff!

"Get away, you — thing!" Eric cried.

Then — *krrippp!* — the vines tore away from the wall. Eric slammed to the stony ground.

Kem leaped at him, but the ground gave way and Eric fell *through* it. Down, down, down he went — straight into the open earth.

Five

The Everywhere Passages

Eric slid, rolled, tumbled, then slid some more until — *thwump!* — he hit the bottom.

"Oww!" he groaned. Every part of him ached.

He gazed about, but it was too dark to see. He felt on every side with his hands. There was hard, packed dirt all around.

"I'm in some kind of pit," he mumbled.

Looking up, he saw a glimmer of

moonlight far away at the top. Very far away.

"Neal! Julie! Keeah!" he cried out.

No answer. Not even the howling and growling of Kem. Eric twisted until he got to his feet. It was hard because the hole was so narrow.

"Galen! Keeah! Help!" he yelled up.

Still, no answer.

Reaching with both arms, he tried to climb, but the sides of the pit were smooth and steep. The more he tried, the faster he slid back down.

"Oh, come on!" he cried. "People! I'm down in this pit! Come and get me —"

"*Spluff . . . muffle . . . pluggh . . . wuff!*"

Eric froze. "Wh-wh-who's there?"

"*Muffle . . . wuggh?*" was the response.

Something was in the pit with him!

Two somethings.

Their noises sounded like words, but of

course they weren't. Then they started scratching.

"They're just digging," Eric said, breathing out slowly. "They won't bother me. They'd better not!"

After a while the sounds died down.

Eric yelled for what seemed like hours.

Why wouldn't they answer? Were they searching Tarkoom for him? What was going on?

Over and over, Eric yelled out his friends' names. His voice became hoarse. His throat hurt.

Finally, he gave up. He hunched up in a ball, tired and achy all over. Exhausted, he fell asleep.

When he woke up, light was streaking across his face. He looked around. Then he looked up.

Droon's sun crossed over the mouth of the pit.

"Holy crow!" he cried. "I've been here all night? Oh, man! Neal! Julie! Keeah! Get me out!"

Still, there was no answer.

Eric felt a sharp pain in his stomach. Hunger.

Of course he was hungry! It had been a day since he'd eaten. His stomach was empty.

Looking up, he tried once more to climb out, but this time he felt something round and hard under his foot.

He reached down and grabbed it.

"Yuck!" he said.

It was one of those smelly fruits he'd found in the garden. Luckily, this one was still in its hard shell. It must have fallen into the pit with him.

He was ready to toss it, when he had an idea.

"The shell is hard and curved," he said

to himself. "If I crack it open, maybe I can use the shell to dig my way out!"

"*Sp-p-pluff . . . m-muffle!*"

Eric laughed. "Prepare to be grossed out, little guys." He took a deep breath, then slammed the shell as hard as he could on the ground.

Crack! The shell split open.

Whoosh! The smell poofed out. It seemed to hit his face directly, like a fist.

"Akkkk!" Eric groaned. In the cramped space, the smell seemed even worse than before.

"*Spliiiiffff!*" the creatures cried.

"I agree!" said Eric, pinching his nose tight.

He picked up the broken shell. The fruit inside was dark pink and juicy. He needed to clear it out to use the shell to dig.

He began to pry out the fruit with his fingers.

His stomach ached again suddenly. The hunger was back.

"No way!" he cried. "I'm not going to eat it!"

But he couldn't stop himself.

Slowly, Eric placed a small bit of the fruit in his mouth. Its cool juice swam on his tongue. Holding his breath, he swallowed. Then he breathed again.

He gasped. "What . . ."

The fruit tasted sweet! It was delicious!

"Raspberries!" he said aloud. "That's it. Raspberries, with sugar on top!"

Eric devoured the entire fruit in seconds.

Then he slurped up the extra juice left in the shell. Then he licked every drop from his fingers.

The most amazing thing was that when he breathed again, he no longer smelled the terrible odor of the pod. All he tasted was the wonderful flavor on his tongue.

"This is the most delicious food I've ever eaten!" he cried. "I've never tasted anything so —"

"Please keep it down," whispered a voice.

Eric froze. "W-w-w-what? Who's there?" he stammered.

"You're talking too much," said another voice.

Two pairs of eyes blinked at him from the shadows. They moved into the dim light.

"Whoa!" Eric gasped.

The creatures looked a little like otters. Sleek brown hides covered their short, slender bodies. Their heads were crowned by bright tufts of spiky white fur.

Their eyes were large and round and friendly.

"You're t-t-talking!" Eric said.

"Of course," answered the first. "It's how we communicate. You seem to have learned it, too!"

"But how can I understand you?" Eric asked.

"The tangfruit," said the second. "Its taste is magic. By eating it, you can understand us."

"And in case you couldn't tell," said the first, "you are now speaking our language. The effect will wear off, of course. It always does. By the way, we are called mooples. We live here."

"Pleased to meet you," said Eric. Then a question suddenly exploded in his head. "Wait. If you live here, you must know a way out!"

"A way out of the passages?" said the second. He began to chuckle and snort.

"Where do you want to go? The passages can take you everywhere!"

Eric's heart leaped. "Up there!" He pointed to the top of the pit.

"Just follow us," said the first moople. "Of course, the way in is never the way out. The passages wind and wind. And . . . here we go!"

The two creatures took Eric through a vast maze of holes. Tunnels upon tunnels. Passages leading to other passages, weaving up and around, crisscrossing each other like a pretzel.

"The passages weave throughout all of Droon," said the first. "Under mountains . . ."

"Under castles," said the other. "Volcanoes."

"Underwater?" said Eric as they crawled by a bubbling pool. "Does that lead to the ocean?"

He wondered if the tunnels led to the dark lands of sorcerers . . . and witches.

"The passages lead everywhere!" said the first.

"And they go on forever," said the second.

"They are all over Droon. You may fall in them again sometime," said the first moople.

"And be welcome, too!" added the second.

"As *she* was, poor pretty thing," said the first.

Eric stopped. "There was someone else here?"

"A child. A girl," said the second. "She had such nice manners. Poor thing was lost, I think."

"A girl was lost in the passages?" said Eric.

The first moople scrabbled up through

the dirt. "We tried to help her. Then —poof! — a big light, and she was gone. Years ago that was."

The other began to snort again. "Years ago! That's funny — if you know what I mean!"

Eric blinked. "Not exactly —"

"You will!" said the first. "And here you are!" He pointed to an opening above them. Fresh air poured in. And moonlight. It was night again.

"Now we must say good-bye," said the first.

"'Bye. And thank you!" said Eric.

"You are welcome anytime!" said the other.

The mooples scurried away into the darkness.

"Strange creatures," Eric muttered. "But nice."

His arms hurt, his head ached, he was

exhausted, but the smell of fresh air drove him up.

Finally, he slid through the opening. Moonbeams lit an empty street of red cobblestones. Kem was nowhere to be seen.

"Of course not," Eric said to himself. "That was, like, two days ago!"

Eric could hardly believe that after all that time and after all that traveling he was only a few paces away from where he'd started. "Amazing," he mumbled.

He spotted the Tarkoom gate in the distance and went straight for it. Then he heard voices.

He darted into the shadows and peered out.

"He was just here, wasn't he?" said one voice.

"Yeah," said another. "Then he was gone . . ."

Eric's mouth dropped open. It was

Julie and Keeah! And Max and Neal and Batamogi!

"Oh, my gosh!" gasped Eric, staggering over to them. "Guys! Guys! I'm here. You found me!"

"Where did you go?" asked Julie. "We couldn't see you for a minute."

Eric blinked. "For a minute? I was stuck in that pit forever! Then I ate the stinky fruit and now it's tomorrow and — I yelled so much! Why didn't you answer?"

Batamogi and Max looked at each other.

"Eric, you were gone for, like, thirty seconds, tops," said Neal. "What's the big deal?"

"Thirty seconds! It was two days!" Eric said.

Keeah frowned. "No, wait. Something is strange about this. Eric, tell us what you saw."

He told them everything that had happened to him. The creatures he had met. What they told him about the passages. How he wasn't the first one from above to have been there.

"Very strange," said the princess. "I think I've heard about these passages somewhere. Magical tunnels that wind around and around until you get lost in them. And what seems like days there takes no time here."

"Perhaps my master has heard of these passages," said Max. "I wonder if they can help us in our mission to stop Ving."

"Good idea," said Julie. "We'd better catch up to Galen. He went on ahead to find a way into the palace —"

"You there!" snarled a strange voice. "Stop!"

Suddenly — *fwit! fwit!* — the sound of heavy wings filled the air around them.

"Hawk bandits!" cried Batamogi. "Flee! Flee!"

But it was no use. In seconds, all seven travelers were surrounded by an ugly band of bird-headed creatures. They grabbed them with sharp claws and pushed them roughly down the street.

"Bring them to Ving!" one bandit cried, clacking his greasy beak. "He'll be very angry!"

Six

In the Court of Prince Ving

"Let us go!" Keeah cried, trying to get free.

But the bandits only gripped her and the others tighter, dragging them down one cobbled street after another until they reached the palace.

"I hope Galen's okay," Julie whispered to Neal.

Neal nodded. "Maybe he can save us —"

"Silence!" snapped a bandit with a large

stomach and broken wing feathers. He glared at Eric. "You! Tell me where the wizard is."

Before Eric could answer, Max snarled, "We don't know! And we wouldn't tell you if we did!"

"Nice crown you got there!" said a skinny bandit who looked as if he wanted to peck Batamogi to pieces. "Ving will like that!"

"And I like that little morsel!" said the broken-wing bandit, casting his eyes on Snorky, who was shivering in Max's arms.

The kids were pushed from a dark hallway into a huge chamber. In its center stood a colossal stone statue towering up to the high ceiling.

It was a statue of a man with a bird head.

"Ving," snarled Keeah, guessing who it was. "Galen said he loves himself. This proves it."

In the flickering light of a dozen burn-ing torches sat the bandit prince. Ving had a large green bird head and an orange beak that curved down angrily at the tip. Two black eyes the size of baseballs bulged on either side of his face.

From the chest down, except for his feathery arms and his sharp claws, Ving was like a man. He wore armor that was deeply gashed and nicked from many battles.

"Icthos!" Ving called, and the bandit with the broken wing thumped across the floor to him.

Eric tried to hear what they were saying.

"Where is the old wizard?" Ving whispered.

"We did not find him," the bandit told him.

Eric glanced around at the huge room.

He wondered how close Galen was. Was he already planning to rescue them? Had he discovered Ving's plans?

The hawk prince sat up. "Release these people! They are our guests, and free to go!"

"Free to go?" said Keeah as the bandits unhanded her and the others. "But you and your men are thieves and robbers of the worst kind!"

Ving hung his head and sighed, his wings rustling. "That was true once, my dear. But now Tarkoom has risen from its ashes. And we have been given a second chance!"

The words sounded soothing, like a bird cooing softly. Eric felt that Ving might not be as bad as they thought. He *did* say they could go.

"We come back to Droon not to steal again," Ving said softly, almost warbling.

"We welcome this chance to live in peace with all Droonians!"

. . . And rob Droon's most precious treasure!

Eric nearly jumped when he heard those words. What? What! He looked around. None of the others seemed to have heard Ving say that.

Ving turned to Batamogi, Max, and Snorky. "Icthos, take your men, and show the Oobja king, the spider troll, and the dog to my room so that they may refresh themselves."

. . . Put them to work down below!

Eric gasped. He glanced at the others.

Again, no one had heard the words!

In fact, Batamogi was smiling.

"Thank you, Prince Ving," the Oobja king said. "Perhaps we were mistaken about you. You are welcome in our village anytime!"

Eric couldn't believe his ears. "Wait —" he began, but already the three friends had been whisked from the room.

Ving spoke again in the same soothing tone. "Now, while we await your wizard friend," he said, "how would you like some food?"

Neal slapped his hands together and smiled. "Now, that's more like it. I am so starving!"

"Me, too," said Julie. "And a chance to wash up would be great, too."

. . . Oh, you'll be washed up, all right!

Eric couldn't be quiet any longer. He nudged Princess Keeah. "What's going on here? Don't you hear what he's saying?"

But even Keeah was smiling as Ving went on speaking about the feast he would give them.

. . . Get that wizard once and for all . . . raid everyone's treasures . . . and terrorize

Droon as we did four centuries ago! Oh, the past shall live!

Eric listened carefully to the words. It was plain that he was hearing more than the others were hearing. But how could he? Why him?

Then he understood.

"The tangfruit!" he said to himself. In the same way he had heard the furry mooples in the passages, now he understood what Ving was *really* saying. Eric was hearing the truth! The truth behind the lies! And it was all because of the tangfruit!

Keeah stepped forward. "Thank you, Ving. A celebration sounds wonderful. You are kinder than we thought you might be."

Of course! thought Eric. Even Galen had said that Ving had magic in his voice.

Ving bowed his feathery head and

cooed some more. "I am often misunderstood, I'm afraid."

. . . It is you who will be afraid. . . .

Ving then began to speak to his pirates in a language of clacks and grunts and whistles.

Prepare the bolt. Once these children and their wizard have been taken care of, we will fire the bolt. Then we shall be part of Droon's present. And its greatest treasure shall be ours! Go!

Eric's blood ran cold as some bandits bowed, then fluttered out of the chamber.

It will be our biggest theft, he heard them say.

Turning once more to the kids, Ving said, "My dear guests! Go, the party is about to begin. . . ."

. . . For my serpents, who are very hungry . . .

Julie grinned. "I love strawberries!"

"And cookies are one of my essential food groups!" Neal added, nearly jumping up and down with glee. "I can't wait."

Ving smiled. "Then let my men take you . . ."

. . . *To the room . . . the floor will give way. . . .*

"I hope you find everything to your liking. . . ."

. . . *Because no one will ever see you again!*

Seven

Room of Tricks

The four children were led away from the giant chamber and into an arched hall-way. Eric glanced around for ways to escape, but there were far too many bandits surrounding them.

"Parties are so cool!" said Neal. "Wait until Galen hears where we went! You hungry, Eric?"

"Um, not really," he replied, trying to grin.

Party! Eric knew they weren't going to any party. He just hoped there was a way to escape.

Icthos, the bandit with the broken wing, stopped at a door and inserted a large key. He threw aside the door and waved the children in.

"Right this way for food!" he said, with a clacking sound. Then Eric heard other words.

Food for the serpents — ha-ha!

The bandits pushed the children inside the room and shut the door quickly behind them.

"Okay, so . . . where's the food?" Neal asked.

It was a small chamber. The stone was as red as the rest of the palace, but stained dark. And it smelled damp, as if from water. All of a sudden Eric remembered what Ving had said.

The floor will give way!

"Climb the walls!" Eric yelled.

"Is that where the food is?" Julie asked.

"Do it — now!" said Eric.

The four children squeezed their fingers between the stones and pulled themselves up off the floor. Just in time.

Ka-foom! The floor split in two and fell away.

Splash! Beneath the floor was a pool of black water. The surface broke, and three scaly heads jumped out and snapped at the kids. *Snap!*

"Snakes!" yelled Neal. He kicked one away with his sneaker. "We're not going to *eat* the food. We *are* the food!"

"Now you get it!" said Eric, scrambling up the wall as high as he could go. "Ving tricked you!"

"But Eric, how did you know?" said Keeah, helping Julie climb up next to her.

"The tangfruit," he replied. "Ving tricked you with his weird magic voice. He makes himself sound good. But because I ate that fruit, I heard what he was really saying. And it was all bad."

They climbed halfway up the chamber walls. The serpents leaped up but couldn't reach them.

"Is there a way out of here?" asked Julie.

"Ask them," said Keeah, looking at Eric and pointing to a pair of green-furred mice nibbling crumbs on a row of stones near the ceiling. "Mice always know."

"Plus, the water's getting higher," said Neal.

The water *was* higher. It was splashing at their feet now, and the serpents were snapping again.

Snap! Snap!

Eric pulled himself up the wall. "Excuse

me, mice? I'm Eric Hinkle. These are my friends Keeah, Julie, and Neal. We were wondering —"

"Will you get to the point!" Neal cried.

Eric frowned. "Sorry. Okay, mice, can you tell us how to get out of this room?"

The green mice began to whisper in his ear.

"Uh-huh," said Eric. "Really? Wow. Sure. And then what? Oh. Uh-huh. Really? Okay, thanks."

The mice scampered away into the shadows.

"What did they say?" asked Keeah.

"Well, they've been here for a long time, so they know everything about the whole palace."

Neal nodded quickly. "Yeah, and?"

"And," said Eric glumly, "there's no way out."

"What!" cried Julie.

"No way out," Eric said. "We're doomed."

Neal nearly choked. "D-d-doomed? Oh, man! I'll never see Snorky again —"

"Or Max!" cried Keeah.

"Or Batamogi!" said Julie.

"Sorry," said Eric. "The mice said so —"

Pooomf!

Fireworks exploded in the small room.

Golden sparks showered over the kids and hissed when they hit the cold black water.

And then there was someone with them.

A man. A fairly young man. With a ponytail.

He stood clinging to the wall next to Keeah and Eric. He wore black boots, a long red cape, and a white scarf around his neck. He had a thin mustache and a short beard.

A shimmering, curved staff was slung in his belt. In his hand he held a short, glowing stick.

He grinned when he saw the kids. "Hi! Need some rescuing?" He pointed the glowing stick at the water. "Wand, send those serpents home!"

Zzzzz! A spray of sparks sizzled into the water. The serpents jumped and snapped once, then vanished into the depths below.

The black pool went still.

"That was awesome!" said Julie.

"That?" the man laughed a cheery laugh, tucking the wand in his belt. "It was nothing!"

"Wow, thanks, whoever you are," said Neal. "But, I mean, like . . . who *are* you?"

The man smiled. "People call me Shortbeard."

"*Short* . . . beard?" said Keeah, searching his face carefully. "You look a little familiar. . . ."

"But you can call me Galen," he added.

The princess gasped. "But it can't be!"

"But it is!" said the man. "Don't you like it?"

Eric's mouth dropped open. All at once, he, too, saw something familiar about the man.

They all saw it.

"Holy crow!" Julie said. "You *are* Galen! You were here when Tarkoom was destroyed four hundred years ago! And now you're here with us! So you're you! You're *young* Galen!"

The young man gave them all a quizzical look. "If you say so . . ."

Then, as quickly as they could, and all talking over one another, the four children explained how Tarkoom had appeared in modern-day Droon, how Galen was now four hundred years older, and why they had come to Tarkoom.

"If we don't stop Ving from changing Droon," said Keeah, "Tarkoom will stay. And Ving and his evil bandits will return to our time."

"You don't want that, believe me," said Galen. "But I just got here myself. I don't know what dastardly deed Ving is planning."

Eric frowned. "I heard him telling his bandits to prepare the bolt. Whatever that means."

Galen chewed his lip and shrugged at the same time. "Bolt, huh? Well, there are good bolts and bad bolts. There's a *bolt* of cloth. That's good. But I don't figure Ving is thinking about a change of clothes."

"Probably not," said Neal. "He's got all those feathers already."

"Right," said Galen. "Then there's a *bolt*

on a door. Could be that. Bolt also means to run fast. But that doesn't sound right, either. . . ."

Keeah and Julie gave each other a look.

"Plus, we have to rescue my dog," said Neal. "And Max and Batamogi, too."

"Ving sent them down below," said Eric.

"Then we need to split up!" said Galen, aiming his wand at the wall. He muttered a word and — *poomf!* — sparks shot everywhere. When the smoke cleared, there was a hole in the wall.

Galen bounded out to a high corridor.

"I'll head to the throne room. Ving is sure to be there," he said. Then he pointed down a shadowy hallway. "The stairs are that way. That's probably where they took your friends."

"I'll go," said Neal. "I hope Snorky is okay."

"I'll go with you," said Julie, smiling at Neal.

"Meet us in the throne room as soon as you can," said the young wizard. "We'll be teaching Ving not to mess with the good guys. And be careful!"

Julie and Neal snuck off into the darkness.

"We need to be careful, too," said Keeah. "We don't want to meet up with any bandits —"

"Ha! I eat bandits for breakfast!" Galen boomed. "Now, come on!" Then he grabbed Eric and Keeah by the hand and shot away down the hall.

Eight

The Bad Kind of Bolt!

The kids ran through the hallways, following Galen's flying cape and glowing wand.

"You're fast!" said Keeah, running to keep up.

"Not bad for a hundred and forty-two, eh?" Galen said, laughing. "Boy, I love this!"

Eric nearly laughed, too. It was funny to think that the old Galen they knew so well had been such a wild adventurer when he was young.

Suddenly, they heard clacking noises. They slowed down.

Before them stood the giant throne chamber.

Eric peered in. "The place is crawling with bandits," he said. "I don't see Ving, though."

But there was something else to see.

A round stone platform was rising up slowly through the floor.

On it stood something big and ugly.

A giant crossbow.

Eric had seen pictures of such things in history books. A bow was attached to a long, straight shaft. A thick cord was stretched far back and locked into place. But this had to be the biggest crossbow ever made. It was as big as a house.

And sitting on the shaft, poised and ready, was an arrow as long as a flagpole. At its tip was a jagged sliver of gold that spat and sizzled with what seemed like electricity.

"My gosh!" whispered Keeah. "I've never seen anything like that. It looks like a lightning bolt!"

"It is a lightning bolt," said Galen, his eyes darting around the room.

Eric slapped his head. "Of course! Lightning bolt! That's the kind of bolt Ving meant! And it's huge. But how will he steal treasure with that?"

"Let's not wait to find out," said Keeah.

When the crossbow was in place next to Ving's statue, six large bandits tugged on a large wheel at the base of the bow. The wheel turned.

As it did, the bow's shaft began to lift.

At the same time, the room's ceiling was gradually pulling apart to show the countryside around the Panjibarrh Valley.

"There is the Oobja village!" shouted one of the bandits. "Aim the bolt right at it! Hurry!"

Eric squinted to see, then his mouth dropped open. "It's Batamogi's village in the dust hills! They're going to fire this huge arrow at it!"

"There must be treasure buried under the mountain," young Galen whispered. "That's what Ving is after."

Keeah turned to them. "We can't let this happen. If that arrow destroys the poor village, it will change Droon forever!"

"It won't happen," Eric said, turning to the princess. "We won't let it."

Galen nodded quickly. "You bet we won't. I won't let these bandits escape into your world."

He pulled the curved staff from his belt. It was made of wood but glimmered with many colors as he swung it back and forth in the hallway.

"Cool," said Eric.

"My rainbow cutlass," said Galen. "I invented it myself. It'll make sure those bad guys never get a chance to use that bolt!"

Keeah glanced across the room. "Eric and I will take care of that big ugly crossbow."

"I like the way you think," said Galen. "All we need now is the element of surprise —"

"There they are!" snarled a bandit from inside the room. "By the door! Three of them!"

"Forget the surprise — let's go!" said Galen. With a single swift move, he jumped into the room, his cutlass whistling and sending off streamers of sparks.

The kids jumped in after him, running for the crossbow, but two bandits swept up into the air and swooped at them, their beaks clacking.

"No you don't!" Keeah said. She skidded to a stop and shot her hands out. "I'll stop you —"

Kkkk — blam! One red ball of sparks and one blue one blasted from her hands. They exploded together in a cloud of purple smoke!

The winged men fell to the floor, coughing.

"What was that?" said Eric, scrambling over to Keeah.

"Um . . . wizard *and* witch powers, I think," she said, blowing on her sparking fingertips. "It would be nice if I could control them!"

Fwing! Clang!

The wizard flicked his cutlass quickly and sent three more bandits spinning high into the air.

When they stopped spinning, they were too dizzy to fly. They fell to the floor — *thud-thud-thud!* — their eyes rolling around in their heads.

"Not so hawkeyed now, are you?" Galen said with a grin.

"YOU!" boomed a voice from behind them. "You will not laugh for long, wizard!"

The three friends whirled around.

It was Ving himself! He flew into the room, his black eyes blazing with anger. He thrust out his claws so fast they seemed to blur in the air.

"We don't need any tangfruit to understand you now, Ving!" said Keeah.

"Puny humans!" said Ving. "You will not stop me! My lightning bolt can destroy whole mountains. It shall destroy the Oobja village, too."

"The furry little guys make you mad or something?" Galen asked, whirling his glittering cutlass around in the air.

"Under their mountain is what I seek most!" Ving snarled. "The royal tombs of ancient Goll!"

The sly smile dropped from Galen's face. "But opening those tombs will release the old dark magic! You can't do that!"

"Watch me!" snarled Ving.

"No, you watch me!" Galen boomed. He whacked at Ving with his glittering cutlass.

Ving dodged the blow and lunged at the wizard with his claws outstretched. "Let the battle begin!"

Instantly, Galen and Ving pounced on each other, and — *clang-a-clang!* — the battle had begun!

Nine

Wild, Wild Droon!

Kwish! Fzz-ang! The large chamber echoed with the clashing of claw on cutlass as Ving and Galen fought.

In the confusion, five bandits jumped to the crossbow and began turning its heavy wheel.

Errck! Errck!

"The village is in our sights," Icthos called out.

"Fire when ready!" Ving shouted back as he lunged at Galen.

"Never!" cried Keeah. She shot a blue burst of light, and Icthos and the other bandits jumped away from the giant bow.

Eric ran with her across the room. They climbed up to the bow. "Let's aim it somewhere else," he said. "So Droon won't be changed."

"Good idea!" said Keeah. She and Eric gripped the wheel.

Kwish! Ving soared over Galen, flashing his claws at him from above. "Give up, wizard!"

"Keep your claws to yourself!" Galen replied. With a snap of his fingers, he soared to the top of the statue and landed on the giant stone head.

Glong! Clank! Across the statue's giant head, over the shoulders, down the arms, and back up again, the wizard and the bandit struggled.

"It's no good!" Eric cried, pulling on the heavy wheel with all his strength. "It won't budge!"

"Fire the bolt!" Ving shouted. Icthos scrabbled back to the bow. He began climbing up.

"Time for some special magic," said Keeah, her eyes taking on a strange look. Eric wasn't sure what it meant. Then she said, "Touch my hand. I think this will work. We can both turn that wheel."

"But it took five hawk men to move it!" Eric protested.

Keeah smiled at Eric. "We can do this. I'm sure we can. If I don't fry us both, I mean. . . ."

Eric blinked at his friend. Then he knew what she meant.

Keeah had begun to master her *other* powers.

When Eric touched her hand, he felt his arms tingle, first with cold, then with heat. Finally, he felt himself surge with strength. "Whoa! I feel really strong!"

Together, they gripped the giant wheel.

Errck! It began to turn. As it did, the shaft moved until it pointed nearly straight up.

"We're doing it!" Keeah said. "Keep turning."

"I'll stop you!" came a snarly voice.

It was Icthos! He had scrambled up behind Eric and Keeah. He reached for the firing lever.

"Fire the bolt!" Ving cried again.

"No!" Eric cried. He and Keeah turned the wheel once more as Ichtos pulled the lever.

Fwung — zwing! The bolt shot straight

up, like a long, flaming sword, right through the open ceiling and straight into the night sky.

"Yes!" cried Eric. "It's going off course! Batamogi's village is safe! Ving won't change Droon!"

Ving shrieked at the sight of the arrow flying harmlessly into space. He turned to the children.

"Bandits!" he howled. "Destroy them!"

"Not so fast!" came a yell from the hall-way. It was Julie. She rushed in with Batamogi, Max, and Snorky. Three bandits swooped at them.

"I'll stop those nasties!" Max chittered. He spun a web of spider silk and flung it over the bandits' wings. They tumbled to the floor.

"And I'll finish the job!" Batamogi cried. He tossed a tangfruit at them and jumped away.

Crack! The hard shell broke on the floor, and the bandits ran out into the hall away from the smell.

From atop the statue, Ving trembled with rage. His black eyes narrowed at Keeah. "Old Goll *will* live again. And to make sure of it — I will destroy *you*!"

With one sudden move, Ving struck at Galen, then swooped at Keeah, his claws aimed like daggers.

"Keeah!" cried Eric. "Watch out —"

All of a sudden —

Poomf! Fireworks exploded in the room, light flashed, Ving was hurled to the floor, and a cloud of blue smoke covered everything.

A figure in a long blue cloak jumped from the smoke. He thrust both arms at Ving, his fingertips sizzling with sparks. It was old Galen!

"Begone, fiend, or you shall know what magic really is!" the old wizard boomed. "Goll shall remain in the past — and so shall you!"

Ving sputtered and snarled and clacked his beak in anger. But it was clear that Galen was ready to strike with all his might.

"You have not seen the last of me, old man!" the hawk bandit yowled. Then he picked himself up off the floor and jumped, and soared into the corridor after his bandits.

"Galen!" cried Keeah, hugging the old wizard.

"Hey, that's my name!" said the young Galen.

The old wizard turned to the young one. A smile crept over his lips.

"Well, well," he said. "Look at you!"

The two wizards studied each other closely.

Young Galen frowned and scratched his short beard. "Strange. You're actually me, aren't you?"

"Rather, you . . . are me!" said the old wizard, tugging on his long beard.

"This is weird and a half," mumbled Eric.

"You can double that," Julie added.

"I would," said Eric, "except there are too many doubles in this room already!"

Finally, the young wizard grinned a big grin and shook hands with his older self. "This is quite strange, even for Droon. But it's nice to meet you, old man!"

"Too bad we must leave now," old Galen said.

"Must we?" asked Keeah. "It's fun just

watching the two of you! The stories you could tell!"

"We must," old Galen said. "Because of that!" He pointed up through the open ceiling.

They could see that Ving's lightning bolt had flown straight up, blazing into the night sky, and was now starting to come back down again.

"It's heading right for Tarkoom," said Julie.

"Correction," said Max. "Right for the palace!"

"Right for where we're standing!" said Keeah.

"We'd better bolt!" young Galen cried. "Before that bolt blasts us! Come on, everybody!"

Eric started to run, then stopped. "Wait. Where's Neal?"

"Oh, dear!" said Max, trembling as he looked around. "We must have lost him in the halls. Poor Neal, I hope the bandits didn't catch him!"

Eric gasped. "We have to find him! We have to —"

Ka — boom!

The sizzling lightning bolt hit the palace.

It blew apart the giant statue of Ving and blasted a huge crater into the floor. Rocks and dust and flames exploded everywhere.

Suddenly, Snorky raced out of the chamber, barking and yelping just like he had that morning when Neal was chasing him. *"Woof! Woof!"*

"Snorky!" cried Eric. "Wait! Not you, too!"

But flames roared all around the room,

rising higher and higher. Smoke filled the air.

The earth trembled and quaked.

And the vast city of Tarkoom began to fall.

Ten

Friends, Friends, Friends!

Fwoosh! Boom! Flaming stones crashed down from the walls. Fire poured out through the hallways and corridors. The city of red stone turned into a city of red flame.

"We must leave before the city is destroyed!" said Galen, pulling everyone into a corner away from the fire. "We must go now!"

"We can't go without Neal!" cried Eric. Then, there he was.

Out of the smoke, Neal stumbled into the throne room. Snorky was nipping at his shoes to keep him moving. Everyone rushed to him.

Neal grinned as Snorky jumped into his arms and started licking his face. "He fetched me!" Neal said. "He actually fetched me! Finally, I have a real pet!"

"Excellent!" said the younger wizard. "Now we can all get out of here. Follow me!"

"No," the older Galen said. "We must go separate ways. You to the past, we to the present."

The young man looked at the older, and nodded slowly. "So . . . I guess this is good-bye?"

Old Galen smiled. "It is. But remember,

while your world has dark days now, they will pass. You must always believe in Droon. And love it."

"I will," his younger self replied firmly. "I mean, seeing you and these kids, I guess I always did believe. I mean, you did —"

"We both did, and do," said Galen Longbeard. "Now go to the storeroom. You will find a flying carpet. You must escape Tarkoom, or I would not be here. But be careful. There's danger."

The younger wizard grinned, his eyes twinkling in the light of the flames. "Danger? Old fellow, you just said the magic word!"

"You and your wild, wild ways!" old Galen said. "Now I know why my hair turned white!"

With that, Galen Shortbeard dashed recklessly across the burning room and into the hallway.

"He was so cool," said Neal. "I mean, *you* were cool, Galen. I mean, you still are —"

Just then — *eeeoow!* — a familiar howling echoed through the halls of the burning palace.

"Kem!" said Julie. "We forgot about him. He sounds mad that we busted up his city."

"We need to get out of here," said Eric. "And I know just the way. The passages!"

"Quickly, everyone," said Keeah. "Fast, fast!"

Eric led them all through the burning halls and corridors of the palace until he came to the garden.

"In the ground," Eric said. "Into the tunnels!"

They all piled into the hole he had fallen into earlier. Eric heard the furry mooples digging far away. He started for the sounds, worming his way through the dark passages.

Suddenly, Keeah tugged on Eric's sleeve. "Excuse me, Eric. This is the wrong way," she whispered. She looked at a tunnel on her left. "We need to go this way!"

"But . . . how do you know?" Eric asked.

Keeah blinked, then said, "I just know." She began climbing through the narrow tunnel. It turned upward. Soon they felt cool air wafting over them.

"I knew it," said Keeah softly.

Suddenly, Eric knew it, too.

Keeah had been in the passages before.

She was the lost little girl the mooples had told him about. She was the girl with nice manners.

Yes, it all made sense now.

It was in the passages, somewhere,

sometime, that Keeah and Witch Demither had met.

It was where Keeah got her witch powers.

Eric knew it, though he couldn't prove it.

And maybe it was in the passages — the passages that went everywhere — that Keeah somehow came to the Upper World. To his world.

Eric knew it all. He would find some way to tell Keeah. He would tell her. He had to. Soon.

"I see stars!" cried Batamogi. "Home! Home!"

They scrambled upward, and the cool air of the valley rushed over them.

Julie was the first one out, helping Max, Neal, and Snorky. Galen and Batamogi were next.

As his friends worked their way out of the passage and into the fresh night air of Droon, Eric paused.

He waited alone in the passage and listened.

He heard the voices of the friendly mooples cheering for them. He also heard sounds from everywhere the passages led to. He heard the washing of waves on a distant shore, the roar of flames, the singing of children in Jaffa City.

He heard the cry of the wind, of ice creaking in the frosty north, the hooting of birds in faraway forests, and the babbling languages of hundreds of different peoples and creatures from all across Droon.

"The everywhere passages," he said to himself. Then, as he climbed up through the hole and into the valley, he slipped onto his side.

And he hiccuped.

"Hic!"

And it all went silent.

The noises, the voices, the sounds.

All were gone.

The tangfruit's gift had worn off.

"Come on," said Keeah, taking him by the hand and pulling him up. "And look at this!"

Behind them, the city of Tarkoom shimmered in the flames. The fire roared higher and higher.

Just then, Galen Shortbeard, perched on a small flying carpet, soared up over the smoke.

"He escaped!" said Max. "I like that boy!"

"He is unharmed, as are the bandits," old Galen said with a smile at his younger self. "They are just being sent back to their own time."

"And out of ours, thank you!" said Keeah.

As they watched, the scene before them shimmered once and faded. Young Galen vanished, and with him went Tarkoom, Ving, his hawk bandits, and the ancient past itself. The valley became still.

Once again, the honey-colored columns were tumbled and silent. The red walls were fallen.

And the great statue of Ving was no more than a mound of dust, blown smaller and smaller with each new breeze from the Panjibarrh hills.

Eeoow! The howling of Kem echoed across the night. It grew more and more distant.

"He got away!" said Eric, looking out over the purple valley. "Where do you think he'll go?"

Galen gazed into the west. "Probably to

find his first master. The one who created him."

"Who's that?" asked Julie.

"Ah!" the wizard said, still scanning the horizon. "You know him all too well. He is Lord Sparr."

Keeah gasped. They all did when they heard the sorcerer's name.

"I knew we hadn't seen the last of him," said Neal. "Even his name gives me the creeps!"

Suddenly, the air brightened behind them.

"The stairs have appeared," said Batamogi. "The Upper World calls the children back."

The small band of friends made their way over the silent plains to where the magical stairs stood shimmering on a hill.

"You have done good work today," Galen told Eric and his friends. "As always, we could not have done this without you. Now, Keeah, without delay, we must find Kem. Find Kem, and we shall find Lord Sparr!"

Keeah looked at Eric, Julie, and Neal. Then she shrugged. "Well, life in Droon is never dull!"

With a final wave to the kids, Galen, Keeah, Batamogi, and Max started across the plains and back to camp.

Eric turned to his friends. "Was that the coolest adventure ever?"

Neal grinned. "Absolutely. Until the next one!"

"We'd better get going," said Julie. "We have a kitchen to clean up. And a living room. And a dining room —"

"Thanks to Snorky," said Neal. He glanced around. "Oh, no, where's Snorky? Snorky!"

The dog came prancing over to the

stairs, licking his whiskers. His paws were stained with bright pink juice.

Eric gasped. "Uh-oh! Snorky ate a tangfruit!"

"It probably won't hurt him," said Julie.

Snorky licked his whiskers again. "Hurt me? It was delicious! But I want to go home now."

Neal's mouth dropped wide open. "Snorky . . . ?"

Snorky trotted up the magic staircase.

"Hmm," he said. "I wonder if humans can learn to fetch cookies. . . ."

The three friends stared at one another.

Then they all raced up the stairs for home.

ABOUT THE AUTHOR

Tony Abbott is the author of more than two dozen funny novels for young readers, including the popular *Danger Guys* books and *The Weird Zone* series. Since childhood he has been drawn to stories that challenge the imagination, and like Eric, Julie, and Neal, he often dreamed of finding doors that open to other worlds. Now that he is older — though not quite as old as Galen Longbeard — he believes he may have found some of those doors. They are called books. Tony Abbott was born in Ohio and now lives with his wife and two daughters in Connecticut.

All the Way Home

Patricia Reilly Giff

DELACORTE PRESS

Published by
Delacorte Press
an imprint of
Random House Children's Books
a division of Random House, Inc.
1540 Broadway
New York, New York 10036

Visit us on the Web! www.randomhouse.com/kids
Educators and librarians, for a variety of teaching tools, visit us at
www.randomhouse.com/teachers

Library of Congress Cataloging-in-Publication Data

Giff, Patricia Reilly.
  All the way home / Patricia Reilly Giff.
     p. cm.
  Summary: In 1941, circumstances bring together Brick, a boy from New York's apple country, and Mariel, a young girl made shy by her bout with polio, and the two make a journey from Brooklyn back to help Brick's elderly neighbors save their apple crop and to help Mariel learn about her past.
     ISBN 0-385-32209-7 (trade)—ISBN 0-385-90021-X (lib. bdg.)
  [1. Poliomyelitis—Fiction.   2. Apples—Fiction.   3. Friendship—Fiction.
4. Self-acceptance—Fiction.   5. Brooklyn (New York, N.Y.)—Fiction.]   I. Title.
PZ7.G3626 Ajk 2001
  [Fic]—dc21

                                                                          2001028174

The text of this book is set in 13.5-point Fournier Monotype.

Book design by Trish P. Watts

Manufactured in the United States of America

October 2001

10 9 8 7 6

BVG

For Vincent Ambrose
with gratitude and love.
Dear Vinnie,
there when I needed him.

And always for
Jimmy, Christine, Billy,
Conor, Caitlin, and Patti.

1

Mariel

*O*utside, the milk truck rattled along Midwood Street, the horse clopping, the bottles vibrating in their cases. Mariel heard it in her dream, just on the edge of waking.

The dream began again: *green lace curtains with the sun shining through, a fine morning; a soft voice reciting a nursery rhyme: When the wind blows, the cradle will rock. The voice stops. The rippling in Mariel's legs starts, her toes jerk.*

It was only a dream, Mariel told herself, only a curtain and a nursery rhyme. It would hang over her all day, though, make her wish for her mother, wonder where her mother was, what had happened to her.

A quick picture flashed in Mariel's mind: a red

sweater thrown over her mother's shoulders, her charm bracelet clinking, her cool hand on Mariel's forehead.

If only she could see her mother's face.

"Mariel?" a voice called from outside.

Squinting, she opened her eyes and looked out at the yard. The apple tree spread itself halfway to the bare board fence, almost hiding the row of houses in back. She loved that apple tree. Loretta, her almost mother, had put a small white fence around it so they'd stay out of its way when the two of them played baseball.

And Loretta was out there now, her hair tied up in a red kerchief. "Hey," she called. "Are you ever going to get up? Want to go to a game today? The Dodgers might just win the pennant this year."

Mariel thought of Geraldine Ginty, her enemy who lived across the street. Geraldine would say Loretta was *razy cray*, that the Dodgers hadn't won the pennant during her whole life. Bums, she called them.

Mariel could almost see the green diamond in Ebbets Field where someone would be mowing for today's Dodgers game. How lucky they were to live only a few blocks away. She slid her legs out from under the soft summer blanket and sat up, still remembering the dream.

Somehow it reminded her of Windy Hill and Good Samaritan Hospital, far away upstate, with the fountain outside and the rows of iron lungs inside.

She closed her eyes. *Sirens screaming, sick to her stomach, legs rippling, jerking. Chest heavy. Someone saying:*

"Hold on, kiddo, another minute, almost there now. Breathe for me, will you? In and out, that's the way. Here we are. Never so glad to see those doors."

And someone else reaching out to pick up her doll for her.

"Don't touch it," the first voice said. "All her things will have to be burned, full of germs. Shame, such a little thing, can't be more than four years old. Polio."

Mariel stood up, her fingers fluttering. *When the wind blows . . .*

What did that nursery rhyme have to do with her mother?

Someday she was going back to Windy Hill.

Someday she was going to find out.

She leaned out the window. "Hold your horses," she called down to Loretta. "I'm on my way."

2
Brick

Brick Tiernan was on his way home, the egg money in his pocket, swinging his baseball bat. Only one road led from Windy Hill to their farm and it was long, coming up the hill and winding around Claude's apple orchard.

Ordinarily he didn't mind. It was summertime, a time he loved: no school, no homework, no studying. Everything seemed easy, even though he was up early weeding, milking Essa, checking out the apple trees, trying to get enough water to them, sweating in the fields, hair plastered to his head. And there were late afternoons to play catch with Pop in the field, or to lie under a tree whistling through a blade of grass.

Soon he'd round the last curve and see their farm.

Mom called it the forever farm. And this time Pop said they'd never have to leave.

But today had a strange feel to it, an electric feel. It was on his skin and in his hair. He could even smell it. Jagged streaks of lightning shot across the sky, like the rays around the Green Hornet in the funnies. The town below had a greenish glow, and their neighbor Claude's barn looked more orange than red. The apple trees were still; not one of the branches moved. The leaves were withered, dying for rain.

But the rain hadn't come for weeks.

Brick raised his bat, trying for a Pete Reiser stance. If they were lucky, Pete Reiser would win the pennant for the Dodgers this year. His father and Claude said it would be a miracle. The Dodgers hadn't come near a pennant for twenty years.

He saw a baseball in his mind, dropping toward him, coming fast over the plate. Pow! He swung, a hard swing, a rounder, feeling the air thick and heavy. He tried it again.

But the smell of electricity stung the inside of his nose. He walked faster, glad he had just a few minutes more to reach home. Supper would be on the table: beans, sweet with molasses and chunks of pork, soft and meaty on his tongue, the ball game on the radio, playing Michigan with Mom and Pop afterward.

The sky exploded with light. The boom of thunder that followed was so fierce the road shook. It seemed to go on forever, a huge angry rumbling that filled his ears.

Another bolt of lightning and in front of him, a tree blew apart. Great hunks of it crashed onto the ground beneath, and branches flew over his head, almost weightless. He dropped the bat and took a step backward and then another.

A smudge of gray came up over Claude's orchard, quickly turning to black, a rolling greasy cloud high above him. The next streak of lightning lit up the woods; every tree stood out sharp and clear. Bits of dried grass burst into flame, and the flame jumped a foot, reaching out to him.

He began to run. The fire ran with him, taking a twisted path closer, then farther away, then zigzagging back toward him again.

Noise crackled overhead, and he thought of Claude's apple trees, and then their own, the young trees his family was counting on to change their luck.

It was hard to keep going with almost no air, almost no breath. "One more hill," he whispered to spur himself on. "A small hill, just have to get myself past Claude's."

Claude was at the edge of his orchard, one hand over his head against the flying bits of flame and dust, the other dragging a hose that was too big, too heavy for one old man alone. He was trying to wet down the trees as the leaves curled up and turned gray and apples popped off the branches; at the same time, he shouted something at the sky, or at the fire, or even at the trees.

Brick hesitated for the barest moment. The air was

I am what is now and not yesterday,
I can be received or given away.

WHAT AM I?

like the apples Mom baked. He re-
he and Pop had planted their own
ning, his face dripping with perspi-
s we'll have our own harvest. *No more*
threw out his hand. "Just like Mom

never save his trees alone. Claude's
ide, wrapping a towel around her
k was in back of Claude, lifting the
l the trees, as Julia covered his head
seemed to dry almost immediately.
e until he could hardly lift his arms.
s tired, too; he could see his large
, red and raw. Brick's eyes stung
throat burned, his mouth so dry
t to swallow.

on forever, the fire, the pulling,
Claude in front of him, Julia in back. But at last he
looked over his shoulder to see the fire veering away
from them, strangely jumping the river, and the sound
of the bells clanging in town and the fire trucks coming.

Finally the rain began to fall. He could feel it on the
cloth over his head and his hair, running down his nose
and cheeks, cool on his upturned face.

Nothing ever felt as good as that water, bathing him
and the bark of the trees and the leaves, bathing Claude
in his straw hat and Julia in her towel, washing the heat
away from the orchard.

3

Mariel

It was Labor Day. All the men in the neighborhood were home. Mr. Boyle across the street sat at his windowsill listening to the Dodgers game. Mr. Ginty waited at the fireplug while his bulldog, Dinty Moore, messed up the sidewalk again.

Mariel leaned against the stoop in front of her house spying on the street through the spaces in between the bricks. Geraldine Ginty stood at home plate, a sewer grate in the middle of Midwood Street. She stabbed at the air with her broom handle, waiting for the pitch. "Come on, baby," she yelled to Frankie McHugh. "Whatcha waiting for?"

From her hiding place, Mariel knew Loretta was looking out the parlor window. Loretta, her almost mother. Loretta's eyes beamed straight down on her head. Mariel could almost hear her thinking. *Stand up, kiddo, let them see Mariel Manning. Get yourself over there to the game. No one in the outfield. How about you?*

Loretta thought she wanted to play. Play with Geraldine Ginty? Play with Frankie McHugh? Mariel bent her head and peered through her eyelashes. An open wagon piled high with old clothes lumbered down the street. Across the top was strung a wire filled with sleigh bells. Benny the ragman sat up high in front, holding Daisy's reins. His hat was a brown fedora with a rose pinned on the band. Daisy's matched, but hers had two holes poked in for her ears. "Rags, old rags," Benny called, batting the wire of bells with his stick.

"Time out till Benny gets by," Frankie McHugh yelled.

Upstairs the parlor window shot open. Loretta's voice floated down. "Dinner's not ready, honey. You've got a while." That was what Loretta said, but what she meant was: *You can play ball as well as they can; there's not a two-sewer hitter on the whole team. Give it a try.*

Mariel squinted down the street; one sewer cover was close by, the next was all the way down toward the avenue. She could hit, maybe even as far as the second sewer, but not when Geraldine Ginty stood there, watching, corkscrew curls bouncing, her hands on her hips, and Frankie McHugh tried not to stare at her legs, which curved like the pretzels in Jordan's candy store.

Who cared? They were both *razy cray*.

But how could she disappoint Loretta?

She pulled herself to her feet, her fingers fluttering like the butterflies that hovered over the lots on Empire Boulevard and zigzagged down the street. She told her fingers to stop fluttering, told herself what Loretta always said. *"Nothing to do with polio, that little flutter. Don't worry, honey. Pay no attention and it'll all go away."*

Mariel even called herself honey, which made her smile inside her head. But she didn't believe Loretta, not for a minute.

Benny's wagon passed her now and she waved to him. Benny was a great guy. He gave everyone rides all over Brooklyn. "Sorry," Mariel yelled to Daisy the horse. "No sugar today."

At home plate, Frankie pitched a blooper that bounced off the end of Geraldine's stick. "Home run," Geraldine shouted, and took off.

Frankie began to screech. "Get the ball, Mariel. Get it."

Mariel reached out with both hands, but it was too late. The ball bounced past her, smacked against a garbage can, and hopped away down the street. She took a step, looking back over her shoulder.

Geraldine came toward her, legs churning, elbows out. Frankie came, too, racing for the ball himself.

They both smashed into her, and the three of them went down.

For a moment Mariel couldn't catch her breath. She

told herself she was going to die. Then she took in air, took it in a huge gulp.

Geraldine scrambled up. "It's a do-over."

Mariel stayed where she was as Frankie looked down the street. "The ball's gone. Rolled into the sewer." He wiped his nose with the end of his shirt. "Now what?"

Mariel looked after it. "We could get a wad of gum, put it on the end of a stick and pull the ball right up."

She blinked at herself. *Great idea. Good going, Mariel.*

Geraldine shook her head of wiry curls. "You must be crazy. First you say the Dodgers will win the pennant, then you tell me President Roosevelt can't walk, and now it's bubble gum on balls."

Both of Mariel's knees were skinned, oozes of red coming. She didn't bother to answer Geraldine. She pulled herself up, nose in the air, and moved out of the street to turn into her alley. She didn't really know if bubble gum would work, but she did know about President Roosevelt. Loretta had told her. The President wore a long black cape so hardly anyone knew; but his polio had been even worse than hers. *"If Franklin Roosevelt could become President, Mariel . . ."*

She had heard it a hundred times. Years ago, before he was President, he'd been strong and powerful, but one summer day he'd come down with polio. After that his legs were useless. *"He never gave up, Mariel. He fought. He got to be President. And you know what he said?"*

Mariel said it in her head. *"The only thing we have to fear is fear itself."* She opened the gate to her backyard. Except for the apple tree in the middle, the yard was a mess. It was a long skinny strip of crabgrass with a baseball diamond she and Loretta had worn into the ground.

And there was Loretta on her way out the back door, her hair black and shiny as the starling's feather Mariel had found last spring.

"Want to hit a few?" Loretta asked.

Mariel closed Midwood Street out of her head; she told herself she was standing on the mound at Ebbets Field. She rubbed her hands in the soft dirt, then wiped them on her dress.

She reached for the broom handle carefully so she wouldn't topple over, then gripped it hard. She had to watch out for splinters but she liked the feel of the wood in her hands. When she held on to something, held it as hard as she could, her fingers didn't need to flutter around like butterflies. They felt comfortable and still.

She narrowed her eyes to size up the enemy, Loretta in her Hooverette apron, grinning as she wound up.

Mariel took a breath and swung. The sound she heard as the stick connected to the ball was the sound of a home run. That solid crack! She rounded the bases as Loretta flew toward the back fence for the ball.

"Better than Pete Reiser." Loretta sank down against the apple tree.

"Well, almost." Mariel grinned. She slid down next to

Loretta, fanning her skinned knees with her hand. "Pete's my favorite Dodger."

"Know what I heard about him?" Loretta asked. "He got beaned by a ball, landed up in the hospital and the doctor said he couldn't even walk." She pushed her bangs off her forehead. Her cheeks were red and she raised her green eyes to the overcast sky. "Whew. Hot."

"Is he out for the season?" Mariel asked, feeling worried.

"He walked right out of the hospital, went to the ball field, and smacked a ball out over Bedford Avenue." She tapped Mariel's head. "Home run, of course."

Mariel nodded. She liked to look at Loretta with her shiny pageboy hair and her Chiclet teeth. Then she remembered. "It's too hot for school to start," she said slowly, trying to sound as if it didn't bother her. "Too hot for Mrs. Warnicki's picnic tomorrow."

Loretta opened her mouth to say something but then she clapped her hand to her mouth. "The potatoes, boiled away again, the pot probably burned to a cinder."

Mariel used the broomstick to get herself up, then followed Loretta across the yard and into the house, blinking in the dimness. She kept an eye on the red-and-green runner in the hall, hopping away from the bits that looked like killer vines.

In the kitchen, Loretta gave the radio knob a quick turn on her way to the stove. "It's the end of that pot," she said, reaching for it with one hand. "Ouch." She threw it into the sink, crashing it into four or five dishes.

Mariel could hear them smash. She put her hands over her ears and grinned as Loretta stood in front of the sink saying all kinds of bad words. Loretta had some temper, hot and quick, but over just as fast.

Already Loretta was picking pieces of the plates up and dropping them into the garbage can. "Don't worry, Mariel. I can bake potatoes in the oven if I have to." She began to smile. "If we ever get a husband in here, we'll have to make sure he can cook." She looked around. "We'd have to clean the place up, too."

"I like the way it looks." Mariel glanced at the countertop under the windowsill. Loretta had plants everywhere, stuck in jelly glasses and cups that were missing their handles. Hanks of wool cascaded out of a cabinet: fire-engine red, electric blue, sunshine yellow. Loretta spent her spare time knitting. She made mittens, scarves, and snoods, and even argyle socks for her only relative, old Uncle Frank who lived in Butte, Montana.

And the walls! They were covered with pictures, most of Mariel. Some of the others were old and curled on the edges, Loretta's parents, when they were young, the father with a mustache as big as a brush. It was strange to think of Loretta young with parents. Loretta was there in her white uniform, and even in the picture her cap was on crooked. In an almost straight row over the table were pictures of Loretta's best friend, Mimi, from nursing school, her cap just as crooked. Pictures of Mimi with her hair long, and then short, Mimi with her husband and her baby boy.

In back of them the radio was tuned to WOR. Mariel could hear the announcer Red Barber's soft voice and the sound of the crowd.

"Dixie Walker's up," Loretta said, slicing a piece of meat into uneven chunks. "Love that boy." She stopped to pop a piece of meat into her mouth, then pointed up to the magazine pictures of the Dodgers they had taped up over the table.

Mariel moved the *Good Housekeeping* magazine aside and looked down at the plate that Loretta slid onto the oilcloth mat in front of her, a slab of pot roast—"a little dry again," Loretta said—and a pile of carrots, cold and crunchy. For dessert there'd be a Drake's cake with white icing that would peel off and melt in her mouth.

Mariel waited for Loretta to sit as Dixie Walker cracked the ball and rounded the bases. She looked up at the calendar: blue letters, a page for every day. She felt her fingers begin to flutter and gripped the fork harder.

Loretta tugged gently at Mariel's hair. "School won't be so bad this year, honey. Wait and see. And just think about that picnic tomorrow."

Mariel *was* thinking about that picnic. Mrs. Warnicki, her new teacher, had sent notes to everyone in the class: *Lemonade, cookies, and games to celebrate our new and wonderful school year.*

Mariel marched a slice of meat around her plate. A schoolyard picnic on the last Tuesday of summer.

"Besides," Loretta said. "We're having company."

Mariel looked up.

"A surprise." Loretta peeled a strip of icing off the cake for Mariel. "Don't ask me more than that." She leaned forward, touching the tip of Mariel's nose with one finger. "Going to be a whole new year, kiddo."

A whole new year . . . like the Dodgers maybe winning the pennant. Outside Geraldine Ginty was screaming about some *razy cray* thing. Mariel tried not to listen. Instead she thought about the Drake's cake icing melting on her tongue, and the surprise company that was coming.

4
Brick

A strange smell drifted in through the kitchen window even a week after the fire, but the smell was different now; it was almost like licorice. He'd never eat licorice again, Brick thought, as he sat at the table finishing his cereal. He could see Pop outside, standing near the fence, his head down, his hands loose at his sides.

"Go after him," Mom said, one freckled hand reaching out to brush his shoulder. "I hate to see him like that."

She stood at the stove, her dark hair curling over her forehead from the heat in the kitchen, her eyes still red from the smoke, or maybe from crying. His mother was an easy crier. She cried at everything, the sun shining on the stream in back of the farm, or a good report card;

she was teary when Pop threw his arms around her to dance to music on the radio.

Brick set his glass in the sink. He went out the back door, going slowly, not knowing what to say to his father, not wanting to look at the orchard any more than he had to. The fire had been much worse here than at Claude's. Everything was black: poor little trees, nothing but stumps without leaves and branches. And even the earth itself was scorched.

"Pop," he called.

His father turned, his hair darker than Brick's, tall, lanky like a baseball player. He almost looked like Pete Reiser. He smiled at Brick, reaching out the way Mom had to touch his shoulder.

Brick opened his mouth to say something he'd been thinking all week, something that he thought of last thing at night, first thing in the morning when he opened his eyes. "I should have come home. If I had been here with you we might have saved our trees."

Pop looked down at him, blue eyes squinting against the sun. "Is that what you've been thinking?"

Brick looked at the oddly shaped tree stumps in front of them. He didn't answer.

"Do you think," Pop said, "I'd have been proud of you for walking away from that old man and woman? They've been like grandparents to you."

"I could have helped you," Brick said, trying to keep his words steady.

Pop put both hands on his shoulders. "You did the

right thing," he said. "You did what I would have done."

Brick could feel something easing in his chest, the pain backing away from him.

"There's something hard I have to tell you." Pop glanced up toward the kitchen window. Mom was at the sink, looking out at them. He waved at her. "Something I don't know how to tell your mother."

Brick looked beyond the orchard to the fields, corn gone, vegetables gone. Last week birds had perched on the feathery plumes, and he'd had to chase the rabbits away from the tight lettuce leaves. But the birds had disappeared, and the rabbits, too, with nothing for them to eat. Everything was quiet and still.

He knew what Pop was going to say. It wouldn't be the first time they had farmed a piece of land that hadn't worked. He remembered when they'd tried a place thirty miles away. Brick shivered as he thought of the river, swollen in the rain, that had edged up over its bank just enough to flood the fields and leave soggy land with the spring seed floating in puddles. And before that . . .

Pop tightened his grip on Brick's shoulders. "There's no help for it," he said. "We'll have to leave again."

"Give up the farm?"

"There's plenty of work off the farm now," Pop said. "Shipbuilding. Planes. We're sending them to England, to Russia, as fast as we can. Maybe if they have enough to fight the Nazis we won't have to go to war."

"But where will we go? When?"

Pop dropped his hands to his sides. "Soon," he said. "Just as soon as I can figure it all out."

Brick wanted to say it wasn't fair. He wanted to say his father had promised this would be the last move. That was what he had said the last time, though, and the look on his father's face, that sad terrible look, made him close his mouth over the words.

5
Brick

Even from the gravel path Brick could hear the rumble of Claude's voice. Sometimes he spoke French to Julia, who answered in a high rat-tat-tat of a voice, or to Brick, who couldn't understand a word but would nod anyway.

Brick trudged around to the side of Claude's house and knocked on the screen. Regal, the dog, waved his tail like a plume and nuzzled Brick's hand.

Last time.

Claude and Julia looked up at him and motioned him inside. It was hot in the kitchen, steamy from pots of this and that on the stove: blackberry jam simmering gently in back, corn bubbling hard in front.

Claude sat in his rocker next to the window, wide

hands up, both bandaged from the fire. He kicked at the chair next to him, pushing it out, but Brick shook his head. "I don't have time." He could hardly get the words out.

"Going now?" Claude said, not looking at him, looking out instead at the rows of trees. Brick could tell that Claude was having trouble with his words, too. And Julia, shaking her head, turned to the stove, lowering the flame under the corn.

"I wanted to tell you I'm coming back someday." Brick glanced out the window, seeing what Claude was seeing: the orchard stretching across the hills on both sides and all the way to the fence that separated it from their own farm. Claude's trees showed the marks of the fire. The trunks were blackened and the leaves sparse, but there were still apples on the branches, red and almost ready to harvest. One thing. They had saved Claude's trees.

"It's a hard-luck place," Claude was saying, "this town of Windy Hill. When we came from Normandy four years ago, we thought things would be better away from Europe and its wars."

Julia answered with a rattle of French, and then, remembering Brick, said, "We don't have to hear that now."

Claude moved heavily in the rocker. "Joseph from over the hill told me that years ago orchards lined the hillside here. Every fall the trucks came with workers to pick apples. Workers singing . . ."

"Claude, we know all that," Julia said over her shoulder.

"I'm telling Brick."

Julia rolled her eyes. "There's no stopping him."

Brick knew Claude was trying to fill up the silence, talking in that loud voice of his so they wouldn't think about his leaving.

"No one comes to pick," Claude said, a deep crease in his forehead. "Julia can't climb anymore. There's only Joseph, who's mostly useless." He shook his head. "And who knows if he'll come?"

"Shhh," Julia said again.

Claude's voice trailed off. None of them said anything; none of them could think of anything to say. The sound of the bubbling water on the stove was loud in his ears. Then Brick heard Pop's whistle. It was time to go back, time to close up the farm and leave.

Julia turned, tears running down her cheeks. "Dear child," she said, patting Brick's face.

He reached for her. Julia was so tiny his hands rested easily on her shoulders. Claude got to his feet as if it was an effort and walked around them to take a book off his shelf. His bandaged hands made him awkward and he almost dropped it before he handed it to Brick. "My book on the apple trees," he said. "It's marked. Underlined. I know you'll use it someday."

"Claude," Julia said. "Your book is in French. Brick can't read that."

"He'll piece it out with the pictures."

"Such foolishness," she said, but she smiled at Brick, her eyes glistening. They both knew it was Claude's best book. Claude thumbed through it all the time, muttering about grafting branches, or pruning, or harvesting.

Brick held up the book. "I'll keep it for now," he said. "But someday I'll bring it back."

"I know that." Claude's voice was gruff. "Luck changes."

Pop whistled again. Brick went down the steps, brushing the top of Regal's head with one hand. He took the path through the orchard, touching the trunks of the trees he had helped save, and opened the door of his own house.

Mom stood in the parlor with Pop, crying the way Julia had. Her freckled face was streaked with tears, her curly hair flattened from leaning against Pop's shoulder. And Pop was holding his face so tight it seemed as if it would crack. He had looked that way since the other night. Brick wanted to reach out and hug him, hug them both, tell them he loved them, tell them . . .

"Leaving," Mom said, her hands out, shaking her head. "The three of us."

Going every which way like the crazy quilt she had made for his bed.

The other night they had sat on the couch, Pop's long legs spread out, Mom with her arm around Brick's shoulders, swiping at her soft dark eyes with a handkerchief, the sound of the radio in the background.

"Remember," Mom had begun. "Remember I told you about my friend from nursing school?"

"Loretta? The one who sent wool scarves and mittens and . . . ?" He tried to remember.

"Yes. Loretta, the best nurse I ever knew. We came to Windy Hill together to work with the polio kids."

It was too much to think about, nurses and polio, and what was going to happen to them now.

"Loretta adopted a little girl with polio," Mom said. "She wanted to go back to Brooklyn, where we had grown up."

"We're going to Brooklyn?"

Mom caught her breath. "Listen," she said. "This is just going to be for a year. For us. For the farm. If we can just do this thing, maybe . . ."

Pop moved toward the window, running his hands through his hair, the pane dark, outside a blur, the burnt trees softer. "There's a factory," he said, "fifty miles north of here. It's good money, making engine parts. Enough money to save some for once in our lives."

"And for me . . ." Mom squeezed Brick's shoulder. "There's a job in Philadelphia with a sick woman who needs a nurse. I can live with her, take care of her, and save every cent."

Brick shook his head. Philadelphia?

Pop turned from the window and sat down heavily at the end of the couch, his eyes glistening. "If you could go to Brooklyn . . ."

Brooklyn. Loretta. Brick's mouth was dry. If he

hadn't stopped that day to fool around with the baseball bat, he would have been past Claude's. He would have been home to help. They might have saved their own trees.

But how could he even think of that?

"I'm going to Brooklyn? Alone? Going to that nurse?" he said. "The one who . . ."

Mom nodded. "I'll write to you every single day."

Pop put his hand on Brick's shoulder. "I can't think of any other way," he said slowly.

Mom reached for his hand. "You'll like Loretta, you'll see. They're not far from Ebbets Field, where the Dodgers play. You can go to a real game."

Brooklyn with a nurse. Brooklyn with a girl who had been sick with polio. Brooklyn.

He had looked up at the picture of the Dodgers, with scrawled autographs on one side. That had been his Christmas present from Claude last year.

And then it was the last minute. The pickup truck was on the gravel driveway; suitcases were lined up in the hall.

Next winter, the house would be cold, without heat. Mice would scurry around the linoleum floor, and flies would pile up dead on the windowsill.

He grabbed Pop's sleeve, the sharp line Mom had ironed under his fingers. He felt as if he were reaching out to someone he hardly knew.

Pop looked down at him and ran his hand over Brick's head.

"We can stay right here," Brick said. "I'll get a job after school working at Butler's. I can even quit school."

The moment he mentioned school, he knew he had said the wrong thing. Mom stopped crying and started to shake her head.

But they knew he wasn't a kid for school. He sat there in the classroom, day after day, all winter long, waiting. He'd look out the window across the snowy fields, thinking about Julia's kitchen and how he'd listen to Claude tell him about the apple trees, the way to plant, the way to prune. And at home, he loved to be in the barn, warm and steamy, milking the cows. Sometimes on a cold day, he'd lie across the back of the broadest one, Essa, feeling her warmth and listening to the sound of the barn wood creaking around him. Essa sold now, the barn empty.

"I could get a job," he said again. He was good with his hands. He had worked at Butler's last summer moving barrels and crates.

"Never," Mom said. "You have to study. You have to read every day. You have to learn. Every single piece of knowledge is important. Besides, you're not going to wrestle with fields that wither away in . . ." She stopped and closed her eyes. Brick knew she couldn't say *a fire*. ". . . in the heat," she finished slowly.

Through the window he could see that a gray car had pulled up in back of the truck. It was the car that would take him to Brooklyn.

"Take hands." Mom reached out to them. They stood in the middle of the room, Pop on one side of him, Mom on the other.

"A year." Pop's voice was high and strained. "One fall, one winter, one spring, and part of a summer."

Brick shook his head.

"Think about Christmas," Mom said. "Somehow we'll be together then."

"And we'll get through," Pop said.

"But the farm?" Brick asked.

"It'll wait for us." Pop spread his hands. "Locked up tight, with Claude to watch over it." He sighed. "It will have to wait. We'll hope . . ."

He looked so sad, Brick thought, no, so ashamed, as if the fire were all his fault, as if it were his fault he hadn't gotten the loan they needed, his fault they had just held on and held on until there was no holding anymore.

Now they were going. *Every which way like the quilt.*

And the time was really up. A honking sound came from the gray car. The man was leaning on the horn.

Mom tried to smile. "We'll start over again."

Honking still. Brick took a last look at the living room. The corner cabinets were filled with the yellow bowls Mom had gotten at the movies. He reached up and ran his fingers over the picture of the Dodgers. And then they were outside.

"You're a good boy," Pop said. "The best. I know you'll always do what's right."

Mom hugged him, rocking back and forth. He kissed her, then climbed into the car, holding Claude's book.

Pop reached inside, touching his shoulder. "I'm proud of you for saving Claude's orchard," he said. "I'll think of it every day all winter. I'll remember it forever."

"Drive carefully, Mr. Henry." Mom looked at the man uneasily. It was someone they didn't know, a man who was doing this for a few dollars.

"I'm in a hurry," Mr. Henry said irritably, taking the money Pop held out to him.

The car picked up speed as it left the farm behind. Brick stared straight ahead at the driver's flat ears, his sparse hair.

The main street of the town flashed by, Logan's ice cream store, the church, Butler's Feed, Good Samaritan, the big gray hospital set back on the hill, and then the sign: THANK YOU FOR VISITING WINDY HILL. COME AGAIN SOON.

It was only then that Brick began to realize something. He sat up slowly, feeling sick. It was September. How could Claude pick the apples with his hands like that, with only Joseph, who was mostly useless, and Julia, who was too fragile to climb? Pick them, and pack them, and take them to the market? No one else was around to help now that he and Pop weren't there. Last year, even Mom had helped, working long hours, her face sunburned, driving the truck.

He had ruined everything. Saved Claude's apples for nothing, lost their own trees. He wanted to stop the driver and jump out, but instead he closed his eyes as the driver turned, taking the road out to the highway. He could hear the sound of the wheels: *Saved Claude's apples for nothing, for nothing.*

6
Brick

The car chugged along, and Mr. Henry, the driver, hardly said more than two words. Brick pressed his nose against the glass, watching the road and all the places he hadn't seen before. He tried not to think of Mom and Pop, or Claude's hands, or the apples that would never be picked.

The land began to flatten out now; the hills were lower. He could see a barn here and there, fields of cows, and then they were gone. Ugly little towns appeared, the houses crowded next to each other, small gray buildings, a school with a flag in front.

The smell of gas from the car made him feel queasy and he closed his eyes, listening to the motor. He kept seeing Mom and Pop in his mind, Mom's dark eyes, Pop leaning over toward him. He kept remembering what Pop had said: *"I'm proud of you for saving Claude's orchard. I'll think of it every day."*

After a while the car slowed down and the driver pulled up in front of a grocery store. Brick opened his eyes to watch him go inside, reach into his pocket for change, and take a Coke out of the soda bin.

Claude. He could see Claude in his mind, too. Claude with his hands in bandages.

Brick glanced at the store window again. Mr. Henry held the bottle up to his mouth, his Adam's apple bobbing.

If only he didn't have to go to Brooklyn. If only . . . And then suddenly it came to him. He knew what he could do. Go back. Go back to help Claude harvest the apples. Everything wouldn't be such a waste then. And he knew something else. That was what Pop would have done if he could. He was sure of it. He reached for the door handle, but the man came outside, the bottle of soda in his hand.

There was no time to get across the road, not even time to open the door.

He sat back as they drove off, thinking about how long the trip was, thinking about how he could do it, when he could do it, how long it would take him to walk all the way home. But the driver never stopped. Finally, Brick dozed, dreaming of dusty yellow movie dishes.

When he opened his eyes, the world had that look of light going, the end of an early-September day. He raised his head.

A city. That was what this place must be. There were reddish-brown houses in rows, paved streets in squares, a huge cemetery with iron gates, church steeples. Brooklyn.

Mr. Henry was talking to himself, slowing down, looking at house numbers. "There." He pointed, then stopped the car.

Brick swallowed.

"Don't forget your bag."

Brick reached for the case next to him, glancing up at the brown house.

"I don't have all day," Mr. Henry said.

Brick closed the car door in back of him. He climbed the steps and put his hand on the bell. But he didn't press it. He waited as the man drove up the street and turned the corner.

Then he jumped off the steps, his suitcase in one hand, Claude's book in the other, running faster than he ever had, running in the opposite direction. He kept going until he felt he had no breath left, coughing, not able to take one more step.

He stopped then, and crouched down in back of a row of garbage cans at the back door of a restaurant. He knew it wasn't a good place to hide. He was too close to the screen door; he could hear people talking inside the kitchen. He stayed there only long enough to breathe easily again; then he went on, going from one block to another. He had no idea where he was or where he should go. And then, out of nowhere it seemed, he was standing in front of a huge building. He looked up to see the sign: EBBETS FIELD.

How could that be? He went closer, moving up to the entrance to see inside: shiny marble floors with markings that looked like baseball stitching, chandeliers with baseballs.

This must be where the Dodgers played!

Wait till he told them at home. Ebbets Field! He'd heard the name a million times on the radio. He'd heard the sound of the bat smacking the ball, the yell of the umpire—"*Safe!*"—and the crowds of people, their screaming like the wind on the hilltop before a storm.

He took a few steps backward into the street to see all of it at once, almost stumbling over the curb. There was nothing this big, this gigantic, in Windy Hill.

He didn't see the police car until it was almost on top of him. If he hadn't run they might have thought it was just a kid who lived nearby, a kid who was on his way home.

But he did run, the suitcase banging against his leg, Claude's book clutched in his hand. They came after him, the car screeching as it swerved around the corner. One of the cops got out, put his hand on Brick's shoulder, and motioned to the backseat.

"What's your name?" one of them asked.

Brick glanced at the laundry on one side of the street, Billy's, and at the pet store on the other, Exotic Birds. He took a breath.

"Billy," he said. "Billy Nightingale."

7

Mariel

*T*his morning, Loretta had twirled around the tiny kitchen holding Mariel's new blue dirndl skirt out in front of her. "You'll look gorgeous," she said, "like Mariel the movie star."

Mariel crossed the street now, the string on the box of bakery brownies for Mrs. Warnicki looped over one finger.

Should she go to the picnic? She stopped to look in the window of Jordan's candy store. The dirndl skirt with its wide band of red and yellow flowers swirled around her and the puffed sleeves of her blouse were tied with blue ribbons. Loretta had even curled her hair with a little sugar water and a bunch of kid curlers.

Loretta would want to know all about Mrs.

Warnicki's picnic, how Mariel liked the brownies, how the lemonade tasted, the cookies, the games they played.

The games. Mariel bit her lip.

At the door, Loretta had given her a kiss. "Remember what President Roosevelt said that time." She held one hand lightly under Mariel's chin.

Mariel had given her a quick nod.

Loretta's voice had floated after her down the steps. "*. . . the only thing we have to fear is fear itself.*"

Mariel had waved back.

"That's what he said, Mariel. Right?"

"I know."

Mariel sighed. She'd have to go to the picnic. But that didn't mean she had to be at the schoolyard the minute the doors opened. Instead she'd take herself over to Ebbets Field for a quick look, see what was going on.

The Dodgers were playing this afternoon, and if she hung around the entrance, she might see one of the players going in early. Once when they were playing the Cardinals, she had seen Pete Reiser on his way into the stadium. He had tipped his hat at her as if she were grown up and had two legs that matched. Mariel turned and walked in the opposite direction from school. Yes, let Geraldine and Frankie hang around the hot schoolyard playing something like Ring Around the Rosy. *Osy Ray*. She grinned for a moment, thinking about what it would be like for such big kids to play such a baby game, but then she felt a quick pain somewhere in her chest. She swallowed, sticking her chin up in the air.

In back of her was a jingle of sleigh bells and the clop of Daisy the horse as the ragman pulled onto the avenue. Mariel raised her hand so Benny would stop, then snapped open her purse to find the sugar cube she had put there this morning.

"Hey, princess," Benny called.

"Hey, Benny." She flattened her palm so Daisy could take the cube with thick yellow teeth, her muzzle soft against Mariel's hand.

"School today?" Benny said.

She shook her head. "Schoolyard picnic."

Benny turned his head to one side.

She tried to loosen her mouth, to make herself smile.

"Maybe you'll have a great time," he said, looking a little doubtful. He clicked his tongue and Daisy started up again.

Mariel waited for the light, then went toward Montgomery Street and Ebbets Field. She was halfway there when she noticed the shoes walking along next to her, keeping time. Black shoes, buffed so shiny you could almost see your face in them.

No one called him Mr. Ambrose. Just Ambrose the cop. His hat was pushed back over his dark hair, his blue eyes crinkling. Blue eyes that saw everything.

Ambrose the cop was everywhere. "Going to the picnic?" he said, eyebrows raised.

Mariel didn't answer. She turned herself around and headed back, putting Ebbets Field out of her mind and

Mrs. Warnicki's picnic in. Ambrose walked with her as far as the gate, whistling.

She stopped at the step and motioned with her hand, a don't-come-with-me wave. He laughed, pulling his hat down over his eyes, and headed back down the street.

Mariel was the last one there. All the old kids from fifth grade were running around the yard. Geraldine Ginty was charging up and down the school steps, her jump rope a lasso over her head.

Mrs. Warnicki wore an orange-ice summer skirt that rode up over her round knees, and there was a round spot of rouge on each cheek. She looked excited to see Mariel. She took the box of brownies, smiling, and put them on the middle of the table with a pile of other bakery boxes.

"Thoughtful," she said. "Very thoughtful." She glanced at the other kids racing around. Already the boys looked hot and sweaty. Their butch cuts were growing in after the summer and their hair stuck up in little points. Mrs. Warnicki turned back to Mariel. "Maybe you could just help me open everything and set it all up."

Mariel smiled, too. Everyone said Mrs. Warnicki was wonderful. And now she wouldn't have to stand against the schoolyard fence watching, pretending she was having the best time in the world.

She took her time with the boxes, putting cookies and small cakes on plates with white doilies. Mrs. Warnicki talked the whole time. "Get to see the Dodgers this summer?"

Mariel nodded. She had been to Ebbets Field every chance she could. Sometimes she went with Loretta and they paid at the gate. The rest of the time she had watched from the grate outside of center field where kids could see but didn't have to pay.

A picture of Loretta came into her head, Loretta rooting through drawers looking for something, talking over her shoulder. "No more bums. No one will say the Dodgers are a joke. We're going to show them all."

"Loretta says they're going to win the pennant this year," she told Mrs. Warnicki.

"Bet she's right." Mrs. Warnicki poured lemonade into a cloudy glass pitcher.

Mariel was down to the last cookie. She put it on the plate and moved a few others around. If only the summer had gone on and on.

Mrs. Warnicki put her hand on Mariel's shoulder. "I'm going to try to make this a great school year," she said. "Different, you know?"

Mariel nodded, glancing at Mrs. Warnicki's red cheeks.

"Little things." Mrs. Warnicki rubbed at her face. "Too much rouge?"

"Well . . ."

Mrs. Warnicki began again. "No composition like 'What I Did on My Summer Vacation.' Maybe something like . . ." She rubbed at her other cheek. " 'If I Could Do One Brave Thing.' "

Mariel could think of so many brave things to do, so many things she wouldn't dare do, it almost made her dizzy. *Brave Mariel saves someone's life. Brave Mariel rescues a drowning baby. Brave Mariel . . .*

. . . finds out about her mother.

She looked down at the plate of cookies. *Her mother.*

She had asked Loretta once. Loretta had shaken her head, looking sad, so sad. "I never saw her, honey. You had been in the hospital for months when I started to work. I tried to find out, but no one knew." Loretta had swooped down to hug her. "Love you, Mariel, love you more than anything. Won't I do?"

Mariel knew her mother must have been at the hospital. Even in that fuzzy time, the machine breathing for her, she remembered the red sweater, the clinking bracelet. *When the wind blows . . .*

She stared at the cookies, thinking of polio. Once she had been able to walk nice and easy with regular legs, and then something had happened—a virus, someone had told her, attacking the nerves that made her muscles move. It made her think of an army of terrible insects marching around inside her legs, eating a piece of this and a piece of that, messing with the On and Off buttons. She shuddered. Loretta had told her that President Roosevelt had spent two years in bed just trying to move his big toe. Mariel wiggled her own toes in her shoes. The army of insects had never gotten that far.

Mrs. Warnicki must have said something, or maybe it was just the yelling of the other kids that made Mariel look up. And there was Ambrose the cop again. With him was a mess of a boy, ice cream all over the front of his shirt. It looked as if he had slept in his clothes instead of having them ironed for Mrs. Warnicki's picnic.

Ambrose the cop walked into the schoolyard, giving the boy a tiny nudge.

Mariel moved around in back of the table, the red-white-and-blue crepe-paper tablecloth hiding her legs.

"This is Billy Nightingale," Ambrose said, his hand on Billy's shoulder. He acted as if Billy were an ordinary boy who had just dropped in to say hello, instead of a wrinkled red-faced boy who was twitching his shoulder away.

Ambrose grinned at Mrs. Warnicki with his even white teeth and gave Billy a nod. "See you later," he said, and marched himself away from Billy and out of the schoolyard.

"Welcome, Billy," Mrs. Warnicki said. "Officer Ambrose told me you were coming." She looked from Billy to Mariel. Maybe it was because Mariel's fingers were tapping on the edge of the table so hard the cookies were trembling a little on their plates.

Mariel didn't even know why she was tapping. Maybe it was because Billy looked angry. She turned her head.

No, not angry. Billy Nightingale was embarrassed. He was trying not to cry. She knew that feeling: a huge iron ball inside her chest, bursting to get out, trying to hold it in so no one else would know it was there, chest closing over it, throat closing.

Without thinking, she stopped tapping, and up went her hand the tiniest bit, and then a little farther as she looked right at him. It was almost as if she were waving, a fluttery wave, a hold-on-Billy-Nightingale wave. But when she realized what she was doing, she quickly dropped her hands down among the folds of her blue dirndl skirt and peered at him from under her eyebrows.

He was peering back.

How could she have done that? She dropped her eyes. But then she couldn't help herself. She took another peek. She liked the look of him. If he'd smooth out his face, he'd be just fine.

And the strangest thing. He was looking at her as if he thought she had a nice face, too. She couldn't remember that ever happening to her before. Not with a kid, anyway.

But that was because he couldn't see her legs. She knew her knees weren't bad, almost matching, round like everyone else's. And her legs were tan now and didn't look as milk-white terrible as they did in the winter. They were bad enough, though. One was thin and curved a bit, the foot dropping by itself when she crossed one leg over the other. And the other leg! It was shorter, much shorter. Even her brown lace shoes with the tassels didn't match. One had a thick ugly heel to try to make the legs the same length.

She looked at the lemonade pitcher. "I'll pour for everyone," she said. She wasn't going to look at Billy Nightingale again. And she wasn't going to move away from the table with those nice long strips of paper hiding her legs for the rest of the afternoon.

8
Brick

Mistakes! He had made so many since yesterday. Mistakes Pop never would have made. Pop thought ahead. *Apple trees need pruning in the spring. Claude said we have to get light in between the branches. And next year . . .*

No next year for their orchard. But there was a chance for Claude. If he went back and helped Claude, it wouldn't be so terrible that their own farm had burned, wouldn't be so terrible that he hadn't been there. He had to get back to Windy Hill. No more mistakes.

Some mistakes he hadn't made, though, some things he had to give himself credit for.

No one knew his name.

Billy Nightingale. All the policemen had had to do

was look at the signs over the stores and they would have known.

But they hadn't looked up. He had gotten away with it.

Standing in the hot schoolyard now, one of the boys had pushed him into a boxball game, pitching the ball to him on a bounce. Brick slapped at it with his hand, heading for first base, hardly thinking about what he was doing.

It had been so noisy in that big room at the police station last night. The clatter of the teletype, one cop calling to another, a phone ringing, made it hard for Brick to think. He wondered how anyone could think. At home the police station was quiet. Only one cop there, one small desk.

It was late when the cop sat down next to him, dropping his hat on the bench. The hat had left a mark along his forehead. He had blue eyes and a small scar on his cheek. "I'm Ambrose," he had said.

Brick was starving by the time Ambrose had cut into a chocolate cake for him, and he ate three slices as he listened to the chiming of a clock somewhere. Nine o'clock. What were Mom and Pop doing now? "Made the cake myself," Ambrose said, and handed him a Melloroll.

Brick had taken the ice cream in chunks because his mouth was so dry, then licked the cardboard wrapper until there was nothing left but the taste of ice cream on his tongue. "I have to walk two miles at home for ice cream," he said, and realized it was a mistake when he saw Ambrose's eyes.

"Knew you were a farm boy," Ambrose said. "I could see it in your face and in your hands. Don't belong in Brooklyn, do you?"

It was the last thing he'd tell the policeman. Better not to say anything, not one bit of a clue anyone could put together. When he saw Ambrose glance down at Claude's book, he had gripped it hard in his hands, but Ambrose hadn't touched it, hadn't even asked about it.

"Listen," Ambrose had told him. "Your mother and father must be out looking for you."

Wrong, Brick thought. They didn't even know he was gone yet.

"They're probably feeling terrible about what went wrong."

That was true. He thought of Mom, her freckles, her dark curly hair, her eyes still red when he left. And he thought of Pop. One night after the fire he had heard Pop crying. He had never heard Pop cry before, never even knew a man could cry. He felt so sad for them both, so lonely for them, but he wouldn't let the cop know that. Instead he reached for another Melloroll.

"If you're in trouble," Ambrose had said, "we'll try to find a way to make it all right."

Brick wanted to tell him he wasn't in trouble, at least not the kind of trouble Ambrose meant. But Ambrose had a face that made Brick want to tell him everything. And Brick was suddenly so tired he knew he was going to blurt out the whole story: the apple trees, and Claude's hands, and wanting to get back.

He had to get back.

Ambrose must have seen the tears in his eyes. He leaned forward, his hand on Brick's shoulder. "You'll feel better if you tell me, a lot better."

Brick opened his mouth. The whole story was ready to come out, every bit of it, and if it had, he'd be at the nurse's house right now with all his plans ruined.

But before he could begin, *"It started on the road from town, the lightning . . . ,"* someone had called to Ambrose.

"I'll be right back," Ambrose had said.

As Ambrose walked away from him, Brick saw it all in his mind: he'd stand on the ladder in Claude's orchard, with apples coming down into his hands, and baskets filling, and Julia and Claude calling back and forth.

And even Ambrose knew when he came back. Brick's face was tight, one hand holding Claude's book, the other holding the arm of the bench. Ambrose sighed, then patted Brick's shoulder. "All right. Let me find a place for you to sleep. We won't send you off to the children's services just yet. Tomorrow one of the teachers is having a picnic. I'll see that you get there."

Brick nodded, thinking he'd run during that picnic, start back.

"Just promise me one thing," Ambrose said. "Don't run yet. Give it some time, a week. Everything will look different by then."

Brick knew what Ambrose was doing. He was buying himself time to find out who Brick was. But the thought of a bed, the thought of stretching out, closing his eyes, made him nod. "All right," he said. "I guess so."

Ambrose touched his shoulder. "Word of honor?" Brick hesitated, but it was hard to look away from Ambrose's eyes. "Word of honor," he said.

9

Mariel

The picnic was over, and Mariel didn't have to think about school for another six days. Besides, she had something else to think about, the company that had never come yesterday.

Loretta had worried about it this morning. After ironing the dirndl skirt, she had taken her breakfast coffee into the living room to look out the window at Midwood Street. "Maybe I had the wrong date." She had rattled her cup in her saucer. "I was sure it was Monday. If only they had a phone."

"Tell me who . . . ," Mariel began.

"It was supposed to be such a nice surprise," Loretta said.

Strange for Loretta to worry. Loretta never worried.

"We've got each other," she'd say, tapping her pink nails on Mariel's arm.

And Mariel wasn't worried, of course not. How could she worry when she didn't even know who was coming? She was curious, though. The guest bedroom off the kitchen, the size of a skinny closet, was all fixed up with the blue chenille bedspread, two pillows, and the extra radio.

But Loretta wasn't even home when Mariel opened the door after the picnic. Mariel threaded her way along the killer vines rug into the kitchen. There was no company in sight either.

Mariel was starving; she hadn't bothered with any of the food at the picnic. She thought about what she'd eat now. One of Loretta's nursing caps was drying off on a towel. She gave the pointy top a little poke, then peered into the cabinet. How about Saltine crackers, and strawberry jam with fat red strawberries and interesting seeds to roll around her teeth?

She took a plateful into her bedroom. Small and dark, the room reminded her of a chipmunk nest she had seen in the Brooklyn Museum. The nest was there in a window: a chunk of earth with tunnels and tiny rooms for food and birthing for a chipmunk family. Safe, just as her room was.

She set her plate on the windowsill and turned on her little radio to listen to *Lorenzo Jones* as she looked over the things on her everything table. There were scorecards from the Dodgers games, a picture of Pete Reiser and Dixie Walker, and one of Cookie Lavagetto. Up on the wall over her bed was her world's best thing.

That was what Loretta called it, and that was what she called it, too. It was a two-dollar bill, brand new, never been used, in a frame just as if it were a picture.

She sat there looking up at it, remembering. *"I'll never get out of here," she had said, talking in between the breaths the iron lung took for her because the insect army was fighting her breathing muscles. "I'll never walk. Never stand up. Never even breathe on my own."*

"Betcha." Loretta, starched and white in her nursing uniform, smelling of spring flowers, had leaned over so close her cap slid down over her forehead. "Betcha two bucks."

Mariel pulled her chair up to the bedroom window to look out at the apple tree with its small white fence and the baseball diamond. Mariel loved to look down at the leaves as they quivered in the least bit of breeze. They reminded her of something, but she didn't know what, something happy, something safe like her chipmunk room.

She was waiting for apples. This year she had spotted a couple of tiny green ones in July, but they were gone now, maybe for a squirrel's breakfast.

She spread a thick dollop of jam on a Saltine and put the whole thing in her mouth. On the radio, Lorenzo Jones was driving his wife *razy cray* with the inventions he was fiddling with in his garage.

Downstairs the door opened. Mariel chewed quietly,

listening. Footsteps. Loretta's quick voice, and a deeper voice . . .

She sat up. Ambrose? Ambrose the cop in her house?

She went to the door and opened it a crack. She could see a piece of the stairs, the broad banister, the hall below. And the top of a boy's head. Red hair.

Was that Billy Nightingale? She swallowed the Saltine in a rush, feeling the soft mush of it in her throat.

Yes. The three of them were standing, almost in a circle, looking at each other: Billy Nightingale, Loretta, smiling a bit, her hand on Billy's shoulder, and Ambrose leaning against the wall. Loretta and Ambrose were talking, as Billy turned and looked up, straight at her.

She shut the door again and leaned against it.

Billy Nightingale was the company?

She could feel the Saltine grow thicker in her chest, making it hard to breathe. It was like the yeast bread Mrs. Stahl made in the bakery, the lump of it growing, spreading, until it took up the whole baking pan.

Mariel had spent the afternoon hiding her legs from Billy Nightingale. She had stood in back of the table forever while the class played Kick the Can and Walking Up the Green Grass. She had stood there pouring lemonade, taking small glimpses of Billy Nightingale when she thought he wasn't looking.

But how could she stay in her bedroom forever?

The outside door closed again. Ambrose was gone. He'd be strolling down Midwood, turning onto Bedford, his hat down over those blue eyes that saw everything. He'd be whistling, a soft whistle with his tongue in back of his closed teeth.

But she couldn't think about Ambrose. What was Billy Nightingale doing?

Loretta was calling. "Mariel?"

She put her hands tight over her ears. *Can't hear you. Can't hear a word. Sounds like the water at Coney Island. Please go away, Billy Nightingale.*

She leaned against the door, hardly breathing as she heard Loretta. "Don't even think about this little mix-up," she was saying. "Everything's all right now. We'll go to a Dodgers game as soon as we can and root for Pete Reiser and Cookie Lavagetto. School will be fine, you'll see."

Billy Nightingale wasn't saying a word.

Mariel went from the door to stand at the window. She stared at the apple tree and shoved Saltines and strawberry jam with seeds into her mouth, Saltines that were going to fill up her whole chest.

10
Brick

Loretta's kitchen was a mess, Brick thought, a great mess. Magazines were piled everywhere, one opened on the countertop. There were other things, too: flowers in jelly glasses, ivy in cups, and knitting needles stuck in a ball of wool the color of apples on Claude's trees.

And over the table Brick saw pictures of his own family: Mom in her nursing uniform, her head tilted. He knew that picture. Mom loved it because her freckles didn't show. There was another of her, too, with Pop, and even one of himself as a baby.

It was the strangest thing to sit there under those pictures, eating melted cheese sandwiches with thick slices of tomato for supper. His mother had never made them . . . warm yellow cheese running onto the plate, buttery toast. They were as messy looking as the rest of the kitchen, but they were terrific even though the crusts were burned.

Across from him was Mom's friend, Loretta. He should be angry at her. After all, she was the one who had figured out who he was. Ambrose had walked him back to the station house after the picnic, sat him down with a pile of food, and she had tapped in with her platform shoes and a face full of worry.

He could have run then; the station house door was open and Ambrose was looking down at Loretta, smiling at her as if she were that movie star, Hedy Lamarr.

He could have run, but there was the promise he had made. A week. And he knew Mom was right about Loretta. He liked her. And there was the girl. He bit at the inside of his cheek. He had nearly cried this morning at the picnic, came so close to it, seeing all those kids looking at him, the teacher standing there, the cop. He'd felt as if he'd burst with it when he saw the girl raise her hand. It was almost as if she knew what he was feeling.

All afternoon he'd thought about the girl waving. She must be a quiet girl; she hadn't said a word, hadn't moved away from the picnic table.

And here in the house he had seen her peeking out of an upstairs door at him. It almost made him smile when he and Loretta had gone into the kitchen, Loretta rolling her eyes. "Where did Mariel get herself to?" He wanted to see her, wanted to hear her say something.

And then she was there in back of him, sliding onto

the chair at the table so fast it was hard to believe something was wrong with her legs. But he knew it, of course. She had been sick with what everyone in the world was afraid of, the sickness that killed people in just a day, or paralyzed them so that sometimes they couldn't walk again, or even move their arms.

Polio.

Brick looked across at her, glad to see her. He felt a little shy, though, wondering what to say to her.

She didn't even look at him.

He waited for a moment, but she fiddled with her knife and fork, staring down at them.

Maybe he had made a mistake. He had gotten through the afternoon because of her wave, but maybe she hadn't waved at him after all. Maybe she hadn't even been paying attention to him.

His plate was in front of him, a blue plate with brown horses runing around after each other, little chips on the edges. He tried not to think about yellow movie dishes, or Mom in the kitchen, or Pop grinning at him in the orchard. *"Our own trees, and we'll stay here forever."* He tried not to think about Claude and Julia.

"This is Mimi's son from Windy Hill," Loretta said.

The girl looked up, not at him but at Loretta. "Windy Hill?" Her voice had a nice sound, high and a little breathy. "The place where—" She broke off, her mouth closed. And now she did glance at him, the quickest peek, but still he saw it before she went back to moving her knife and fork around.

Loretta nodded. "Good Samaritan, honey, and outside of that, there are orchards and a little town." Loretta began to talk about Mimi and about St. Catherine's Hospital right there in Brooklyn, where they had met at nursing school. She talked about Windy Hill, where they had gone to take care of kids with polio. "I was a little girl when I first learned about polio," she said. "It was 1916. Nine thousand kids in New York had polio that summer. Everyone was afraid; no one knew how it started." She sighed. "No one knows now." She shook her head and smiled at Mariel. "I found you right there in an iron lung twice your size and knew you were going to be my family."

Then Loretta began to talk about baseball. "We'll go to the game on Saturday and see the Dodgers take on the Giants." Her head was to one side, and she tapped his shoulder. "Your mom wrote that you like the way Pete Reiser plays." She shook her head. "That kid throws himself into everything, walls, balls, bats."

Brick took another look at the girl across from him. Her head was bent over her cheese sandwich now, so that all he could see was her fine hair. It was the color of sand, and the part in the middle was slightly crooked.

He had watched the girl in between playing boxball and wolfing down a couple of brownies. He had stared out the gate, too: not a field, not a dirt path, not even a tree in sight, just a row of brown houses on the other side of the street.

"You should have seen the Dodgers play the Giants," Loretta said. "Right, Mariel? Wonderful."

He could see she wanted Mariel to talk, but the girl wasn't having any of it. She pushed her cheese sandwich around her plate, her fingers fluttering a little, her eyes on the radio on the counter as if she were listening, except that the radio wasn't on.

He had to get out of there, he told himself for the hundredth time. He took a huge bite of his sandwich, wondering about his promise to Ambrose the cop. A week. And would Ambrose be there at the end of that time, watching him, making sure he didn't run?

Loretta went on. "The next couple of days will make all the difference. We've got three games with the Giants coming up next weekend. Our enemies. And then the Dodgers will be on the road. Wouldn't it be something if they won enough to get the pennant? The first one in twenty years."

Before he could stop himself, he blurted out, "How far is it from Brooklyn to Windy Hill?"

Loretta stopped with her fork halfway to her mouth. "Oh, Brick. It must seem so far away," she said.

Across the table the girl's head came up. "Brick?"

He knew what she was thinking. The teacher had called him Billy Nightingale a hundred times. *"Everyone, this is Billy Nightingale. Want some more lemonade, Billy? Cupcakes, Billy Nightingale?"*

He cleared his throat.

"Brick," said Loretta. "His nickname."

Mariel looked at him for just a moment more. An angry look? A look as if she thought he was crazy? Then she bent her head over her plate again.

And even though Loretta talked for the rest of the meal, and over her shoulder while she did the dishes, Brick didn't hear one word she was saying.

11
Mariel

*T*he rest of the week was terrible. Loretta had taken time off, and every morning she stuffed cream-cheese-and-jelly sandwiches and cookies into brown paper bags for them to take to Breezy Point or Coney Island. The trips should have been wonderful, but Mariel lagged behind, not saying a word to Brick.

On Saturday, before Brick came down for breakfast, Loretta showed Mariel the tickets for the game at Ebbets Field. Then she put them down on the table. There were spots of color in her cheeks. "What's the matter with you anyway, Mariel? Good grief!" Ordinarily Mariel might have laughed. It was funny to see Loretta angry about a spot on her nursing cap, or a pot that burned, or rain on a day for a picnic. But Loretta was never angry at her.

"Why aren't you friends with Brick?" Loretta said. "I thought this would be such a wonderful year for you."

Mariel put her hand up to her head. "I just have to get my hair clip." And before Loretta could say another word, she was on her way to her bedroom to find the barrette she hadn't worn in a year.

She stopped in front of the mirror to take a look at her legs. Candles that had been left too close to the stove, curved instead of tall and straight. And Loretta thought he'd want to be friends. She felt a burning in her throat, and a quick feeling of *wouldn't it be nice to be Brick's friend*, as she found the barrette in the back of her dresser drawer and ran it through her hair, feeling scratchiness as she clipped it in.

She decided she wasn't going to bother about Brick Tiernan today. She was going to wear the new overalls with crisscross straps and red buttons that Loretta had bought for her on sale at Loeser's department store. Brick Tiernan wouldn't see her legs and neither would anyone else.

They left early. "I've got a bag of plums because we'll be thirsty," Loretta told them, "and enough money from the penny jar to treat to ice cream."

The seats were wonderful, so close to the first-base line that Mariel could lean on the iron bar in front of her and watch Dolph Camilli at first, and Curt Davis, the pitcher, as he scuffed up the soft dirt around the pitcher's mound.

It was an easy first inning, a boring inning with the

Giants' pitcher, Fiddler McGee, putting the Dodgers out, one two three. Curt Davis did the same to the Giants.

Mariel could see Brick out of the corner of her eye. He leaned forward, too, telling Loretta over his shoulder, "My father always wanted to see a game, and my friend Claude, too."

And even though she had promised herself she wouldn't think about it ever again, Mariel remembered the picnic on Tuesday, remembered that they had looked at each other . . . had they really looked at each other? . . . and she had thought they might be friends.

And then it was the second inning, the Dodgers were up, and Camilli walloped a pitch far above the scorecard clock all the way onto Bedford Avenue. By the end of the inning Lew Riggs had come home, too. Everyone was standing and cheering. And Brick, forgetting it was Mariel, pounded her on the shoulder.

But that wasn't the most exciting inning of the game. Not even watching Pete Reiser slide home when they knew the Dodgers were going to win, really win against the Giants' one unearned homer, was the most exciting. It was toward the end of the game she'd never forget. And it was Pete Reiser who would do it for her.

She had a mouthful of plums, she and Brick had even grinned at each other when Dixie Walker had a screaming fight with the umpire, a quick grin, and they both leaned forward watching as Pete Reiser came to the plate again.

He took powerful swings in the air as the pitcher wound up. Pete was batting wild, the first ball out of play on the first-base line, coming close to the stands, and then the second even closer, bouncing off the wall with a *pock* that rang in Mariel's ears. But it was the next wallop that made the difference. It popped up high, still far wide of first, and Mariel could see it coming, round and white, spiraling through the air toward her, with everyone in the stands, heads stretched, necks stretched, arms stretched, trying to see where it would go.

All of them wanted to make the catch, Mariel most of all, even though she could feel herself losing her balance, knowing she had to reach out and grab the iron bar in front to hold herself up, instead of reaching for the ball.

She wanted that ball, she could see it in her mind, raising her hands almost in slow motion as she felt her legs go out from under her, and it was coming closer, an arc straight down the first-base line, veering toward her, high but dropping, dropping as she tried to stay on her feet for one more second.

She caught a glimpse of Brick's arms, too, up, ready to make the catch, but saw them in a blur, knew he wasn't going to be fast enough because it was her ball.

She braced herself against the iron bar, both hands up, and the ball dropped, almost as if Pete Reiser had dropped it there on purpose, and it was hers, a hard stinging ball, her ball, in her hands, and she held on, feeling the pain of it in her wrists and in her arms.

Her ball.

And Loretta next to her screaming, and screaming, and Brick, too, both of them grabbing her shoulders, holding her up, and smiling, laughing, the three of them, the people around them clapping, somewhere up in back, Hilda the fan clanging her cowbell, and Pete Reiser, looking up at her, raising his hand in a little salute.

12

Brick

Loretta never stopped talking on the way home. "It was the best day I've had in years," she said, "to see Brick at his first game! To see Mariel catch that ball." She shook her head. "And the Dodgers beat the Giants."

Mariel handed the ball to Brick to look at, and he could see the difference it had made. She was talking now, almost as much as Loretta, watching as he turned her ball in his hand.

"Know why they call them the Dodgers?" she asked as they stepped off the curb crossing Bedford.

"Dodging balls?" he asked.

She shook her head. "It's because of all the trolleys in Brooklyn. Everyone has to dodge them. So . . ."

He nodded, still looking at the ball, the smoothness of

the leather, the red stitching. Usually he hated to write letters, but he couldn't wait to write and tell Mom and Pop about the game and the trolley story. He felt that sharp pain under his ribs, missing them, wishing they had been there to see the game. And then a second pain: Claude. How could he have forgotten Claude this afternoon? How could he have forgotten about going home?

Supper was late because Loretta had burned the hamburgers to little black pieces of coal, and at the last minute had made tomato and lettuce sandwiches. "Can't mess those up," she said.

"Good score today, four to one," Mariel said. "And how about that fight between Dixie—"

"And the umpire," Brick said. "What was his name?"

"Magurk," Mariel said, licking the mayonnaise off her fingers.

And then Loretta blasted water and soap into the sink until the bubbles frothed over the edge. "Go out in the back, both of you. Take a plate of chocolate chip cookies. They're wonderful, if I do say so, not one bit burned, a miracle." She winked at them. "Leave me to the dishes, the radio, and my feet on a pillow."

Brick took the last bite of his sandwich, reached for a couple of cookies, still warm from the oven, and pushed back his chair, glancing over his shoulder at the door.

He went outside and stopped. In front of him was an apple tree with a tiny white fence around it. It was smaller than the apple trees at home, and not an apple in sight. What would Pop say about an apple tree in Brooklyn? What would Claude say?

Mariel followed him outside. He had been so glad for her all afternoon, the look of surprise when she had caught that ball, the look of wonder. Somehow it had made them friends.

They sank down on the weedy grass, leaning back against the apple tree's little fence.

"Billy Nightingale?" She picked up a thready bit of bark from the apple tree and began to shred it in her hands. Her head was down again, the crooked part in her hair showing.

"That was from a sign on the laundry and a pet shop. . . ."

She looked up, grinning. "Billy's. Yes."

Then he heard the sound of sleigh bells outside the fence. It made him think of winter in Windy Hill, of the apple trees with snow covering their branches like blankets.

"It's the ragman on his way home. He's late tonight," Mariel said. "He lives in Manhattan somewhere." She put the bits of bark in a little pile. "Almost on his way home. He has to stop at Jordan's candy store. Daisy takes him there every night for water and a candy bar."

And then they were talking, both of them in a rush, about the game and Breezy Point on Thursday, and even Ambrose, who had come yesterday to see how he was doing. As she reached for one of his cookies, he thought about how easy it was to talk to her, the easiest thing he had ever done. At school in Windy Hill he had fooled around with the other boys, played ball with them, talked about the Dodgers, but not the girls. They were always playing jump rope near the fence, or talking in tight little knots, and he never knew what to say to them.

He began slowly. "There was a fire. It hadn't rained for weeks. Everything was dry, bone dry, and just waiting for that summer lightning to hit." He took a breath. It was so good to talk about it, so good to tell someone.

She looked up at him.

"Almost everyone moved away from Windy Hill." He shrugged. "The Depression is still bad, and there are no loans from the bank to pay for equipment or fertilizer. Most of the people just packed up and left their farms." He frowned.

She sat there unmoving, the cookie crumbling in her hand.

"The fire took our trees and our corn." He spread his hands. "Only Claude is left now, and he won't be able to hold out for the winter."

He sighed, thinking of Pop's hand on his shoulder, telling him he was proud that he had saved the orchard. Saved it for just a few weeks. Poor Claude.

How could he tell Mariel what Claude was like? Claude wearing the old blue sweater Julia had knitted for him, the straw hat covering his gray hair, the way he knew the trees, touching them as if they were his family? How could he tell her how loud Claude was, and how soft and gentle Julia was and how she tried to keep Claude calm?

He told about himself instead. "I'm not good in school." He shrugged. "Terrible at reading, can't sit still for it. Okay in arithmetic and science, though. Claude said I had to be, needed that for the trees."

"Claude," she said.

"I have Claude's book," he said. "Everything about apple trees is in that book. Everything in the world. It's in French, though."

"Do you know French?"

"Of course not." They were grinning at each other now, leaning forward. Then he shook his head. "Claude's hands were burned in the fire." Brick didn't even want to think about how his hands had looked afterward. "He'll never be able to harvest. There's only Joseph to help now. It won't be enough."

Mariel looked up at the apple tree, then she leaned forward. "Couldn't you go back? Couldn't you harvest for him?"

13

Mariel

"I'll help you," she said, even though she couldn't believe she was saying it. She could see how it would be, how he'd get himself back to the orchard, back to Claude, and harvest the apples.

She looked down at the new blue overalls hiding her legs. Now that she thought about it, Brick hadn't paid any attention to her legs all week. Not like Geraldine and Frankie and the kids in school who pretended not to look but couldn't help themselves.

A quick picture in her mind. *Geraldine Ginty standing in front of her outside the house when she had come to Brooklyn years ago. "Want to see the apple tree?" Mariel had asked.*

Mrs. Ginty from her window: "Get over here, Geraldine,

right now." And then in a loud whisper as Geraldine backed away from her, "Want to catch polio?"

Geraldine had run across the street, darting out of the path of the milk wagon, turning back at the curb to stare at her.

Loretta had stormed outside then to the middle of the street, her face red. "She's not contagious, Mrs. Ginty, not for a long time."

Mrs. Ginty's face was flushed, her hand to her mouth.

"Any kid can get polio, anyone in the whole world, and the contagion is in the beginning, not later, not now. Mariel's fine now. She's terrific."

"Sorry," Mrs. Ginty had said. "I'm really——"

"I hope so," Loretta said, "because this child of mine has been through so much."

"I'm really . . . ," Mrs. Ginty had begun again, and had crossed the street to Loretta and spoken in a low voice. "I am sorry. It's just that I'm always afraid. If only we knew where it came from. Someone said it's from the water, so we don't go to the beach. Someone said flies bring it on fruit, so we don't . . ."

Loretta put out her hand. "It's all right. Just——" She had broken off. And Mariel, looking at Geraldine still across the street, had stuck out her tongue. Just for a second.

She wondered now if Geraldine remembered that.

Loretta had taken her hand then and inside had showed her how to knit. "We'll make gorgeous mittens, sky blue and pink. Don't worry about the Gintys. Knit one, purl one . . ."

"I had polio," Mariel told Brick at last.

He was nodding. He knew.

"I can't remember before that, only being sick in Windy Hill, in an iron lung because I couldn't breathe, then coming to Brooklyn with Loretta." She swallowed. "No one could find my mother."

He didn't answer, but she could see his head go back just the slightest bit. And then she had another thought. Suppose he hadn't noticed her legs? Suppose he was so worried about Claude that he hadn't even thought about her or what she looked like?

But if he was really going to be her friend . . .

She had to take a chance. "There's a stone carving of a king . . . ," she began slowly, picking her words. "It was back in ancient times, and his leg was thin and curved. Loretta showed it to me. He was walking with a stick."

She could see his eyes, never looking down at her legs, looking at her face.

"So they know that polio has been around for thousands of years. And my legs are like that, too." She stopped, feeling as if she couldn't breathe, while she waited for him to say something.

"My mother told me President Roosevelt had polio—" he began.

She didn't wait for him to finish. "That's what I told Geraldine Ginty!"

"The President has to crawl upstairs, he can't take one step alone," Brick said at the same time. "And he's one of the greatest presidents we've ever had."

"That's what Loretta says." Mariel wanted to stand up, wanted to twirl around the apple tree, holding the bark . . .

A friend. She had a friend.

"I was in a room with green lace curtains," she said, trying to think of how she could explain it. "The curtains blew in the wind and I could see the sky—" She broke off. "If I find that room, I'll know what happened to my mother."

He was staring at her, looking at her so hard, listening. She raised her shoulders just a bit, trying to smile. "You have to go home," she told him. "You have to go home right away and save the apples."

He shook his head. "I promised Ambrose I'd stay for a week."

She thought about it. "All right," she said firmly. "But not one day longer."

He grinned at her, red hair down over his forehead. "You're tough. Tougher than I am."

She smiled at him. Tough? She was afraid of everything all the time. "I am tough." She crossed her fluttering fingers, hoping he didn't see.

Loretta came to the door. "Hey, kids. It's getting late."

A few minutes later, Mariel stood at her window in her chipmunk-safe bedroom. Outside, the streetlights cast a warm orange glow across the yards. She thought about Brick living in Windy Hill near the hospital, her fingers fluttering against the screen. *Loretta looking up from her knitting, yellow wool spilling onto the chair next to her.* "One day you'll go back to Windy Hill, sweetie. One day when you're all grown up. You'll see the hospital, and the hall where we turned and waved goodbye."

Mariel closed her eyes, thinking about her own mother. *Red sweater across her shoulders, bracelet clinking . . . when the wind blows, the cradle will rock . . .*

14
Brick

It was hot and sticky. Overhead, clouds raced along, one piled on top of another. They started down Midwood Street and turned back to wave to Loretta. Claude's book was tucked under Brick's arm, and they carried bag lunches just the way he would have at home.

The difference was they weren't going to school.

He was careful to move slowly. He didn't want to make it hard for Mariel to keep up, even though she moved faster than he thought she could.

And she certainly thought faster than he did.

"No school today," she had whispered over the breakfast table.

He had glanced down the hall, too. Loretta was

nowhere in sight, but he could hear her singing that Glenn Miller song. He remembered Mom and Pop dancing in the kitchen, the radio turned on loud, his father swinging his mother out, barely missing the table, and then back to him.

Going home, Brick thought, *going home today*. But how? He tried to push the worry down deep inside his chest. What he was going to do was almost like the game they used to play at birthday parties, Pin the Tail on the Donkey. Someone spun you around blindfolded, gave you a little push, and you were supposed to find the right way by yourself.

He didn't even know the way out of Brooklyn.

"I have to put you somewhere this morning," Mariel said, leaning across the table, sounding as if he were a package. "A place where Ambrose won't find you."

He swallowed a bite of Wheaties, wondering what she was talking about, but Loretta came into the kitchen, her nurse's cap perched on her head, the point off center.

"The Dodgers are taking on Chicago today," Loretta said. She looked out the window, head turned. "Wonder if it's going to rain there? Wonder if it's going to rain here?"

It is going to rain, Brick thought as he waited with Mariel to cross Bedford Avenue.

"The hardest part," Mariel said, "is the next block. Ambrose is always where you don't want him to be." She grinned at him. "He'll be lurking around the park like the Shadow on the radio. But I know a place . . . He's never caught me there, not once in all this time."

Brick shook his head. "I don't understand."

"You'll stay in the park while I go to the library." Mariel stopped walking for a moment. "I'll find directions to Windy Hill for you."

She thought of everything.

"There's a book of maps on the back table," she said. "It's like connecting the dots, going from one place to another, you know? That's all it is."

He felt a weight come off his chest.

"And if I get caught," she said, limping along next to him again, her face turned up, "Ambrose will just walk me to school. I'll skip out again at lunchtime."

They crossed Washington Avenue, hurrying, as she glanced back and then went on again. He could see what an effort it was for her, the limp growing stronger, her face a little pale under her freckles.

He followed her, houses on one side, not as pretty as the ones on Midwood Street, the green trees of a park on the other. A few black cars were parked here and there; a few kids passed them on the way to school. Then in front of them were the gates to the park.

"Prospect Park," Mariel told him. "An everything place, like the everything table in my bedroom. Woods and parade grounds and a lake with a house almost like a castle, even a merry-go-round." She pointed. "And another kid playing hookey. See there. He doesn't go to school some days either."

Brick looked over at him. The boy was sitting on a bench, not paying attention to them, it seemed, not paying attention to anything, but then he raised his hand in a half wave.

Mariel kept going around the path, then leaning closer, almost whispering. "And there's my place." She gave his arm a little tug, leading him now, going as fast as she could.

A few minutes later she stopped. "Here."

"But what is it?" he asked.

"A band shell. They play music here on Sundays," she said. "It's the best hiding place." She held up one hand. "I think I felt a drop of rain."

How could he hide without someone seeing him? he wondered.

It was as if she knew what he was thinking. "Once Ambrose walked around it looking for me," she said. "I just kept going ahead of him, crouching down, just as if I were a merry-go-round." She fanned her face with one hand. "Hot, isn't it? Someday when I'm grown up, I'm going to tell him."

Brick shook his head. "Won't he be angry?"

"I'll be grown up then," Mariel said, sinking down on the grass. "But I don't think so. I think he'll laugh." She bit her lip. "Ambrose is"—she raised her shoulders—"there when you need him."

He sank down next to her, looking up at the gray sky through the leaves of a bushy little tree, putting Claude's book inside his bag of lunch, out of the rain.

He ran his hands through the grass, feeling the spiki-
ness of it, the damp earth underneath. He told her about
the river in Windy Hill on a day like this, the trees leaning over to dip their branches into the warm shallow water, the gurgling sound of the river as it ran across the
rocks, the pattering of the rain on the leaves.

He was hit with a wave of homesickness, remembering his bedroom window, the apple trees outside in neat
paths, Mom downstairs in the kitchen, laughing with
Pop.

Home.

"Listen, Billy Nightingale. Brick?" She turned her
head. "For your hair?"

He raised one shoulder. "It's the color of the bricks
in our icehouse."

For a moment they sat there, the rain pattering
against the side of the band shell. He watched her fingers tap on her dress and then she clasped her hands together. He wondered what she was thinking.

"I'll go to the library now," she said. "When I come
back you'll know the way to Windy Hill."

15

Mariel

Mariel passed the candy man on the way to Grand Army Plaza. He was bent over, the weight of his square pack on his back, an umbrella over his head. He tossed Mariel a peppermint and she managed to catch it with one hand. A little kid, too young for school, stood under an awning on one of the stoops. He held out his hands. "Hey, girlie," he said. "How about sharing?"

She looped the peppermint toward him, watched him scramble for it, then turned the last corner and went up the library steps, holding on to the railing, slick with rain.

A memory. *The green lace curtain clutched in her hand. Someone had tossed a piece of candy to her. But her head felt as if it had been stuffed with something thick and damp like rolls of cotton. So she didn't reach out and the candy fell in an arc down and down. . . .*

Inside, the library was cool and dim, the squares of windows streaming with rain. In the center of the bulletin board was a picture of two kids smiling, and a sign: FRIENDS GO BACK TO SCHOOL.

Mariel ran a finger over the words. She had a friend for the first time in her life. She practiced saying it in her head. *Friend. My friend.*

No one would ever know about it. By this afternoon he'd be gone.

She'd know, she told herself, she'd know forever.

She skittered past the desk. The librarian's head was bent. She didn't even look up to see a girl out of school.

Mariel went down the long aisle filled with books on both sides. She knew the library, the children's section, the adults'. She had spent years here. *Everyone out playing. Mariel has germs.*

On Saturday afternoons, she had looked at the books of world maps with their strange names: Ceylon, Singapore, Burma. And the maroon one of her own country, a page for each state: Maryland, Montana, Nebraska. She had flipped through, getting closer to her state all the time.

And there it was, the triangle of New York.

Windy Hill was just a small dot on the top. The first time she had looked it up, it had taken forever to run her fingers from one corner to the other. And when she finally spotted it, she had shivered. It was almost as if she were there in Good Samaritan Hospital, and back even farther, somewhere with the green lace curtains trembling in the breeze.

She had picked up a pencil that she found on the table and drawn a line under Windy Hill, a line so faint that no one would see it, but she'd know it was there.

"I hope you're not marking up that book," the librarian had said that day, standing in back of her suddenly, sounding disappointed.

Mariel had erased the line, but there was still the tiniest smudge so she could always find it.

The book was waiting for her now, ready to show her how Brick would get home.

She peered around the library stacks, making sure the librarian was still too busy to wonder why a girl was at the library instead of in a classroom. Then she reached for the book.

It didn't take her long to realize that Brick wasn't going home. Not today, and not soon, certainly not soon enough to help his friend Claude harvest apples.

Her disappointment for him was so great she could feel it in her throat and in her chest. She pored over the map book with its spidery lines, counting off the miles in her head and then on a piece of paper that she found on the table. More than two hundred. Certainly more.

She traced it with her finger. Over a bridge from Brooklyn to Manhattan. Another bridge. Then up, and a zigzag and farther up, following the Delaware River.

It wasn't a place you could walk to easily. If you

walked even ten miles a day . . . could a person walk that far? she wondered . . . it would take almost a month.

And where would he sleep?

Where would he find something to eat?

And by the time he reached Windy Hill, a place much colder than Brooklyn, wouldn't the apples be frozen?

She thought of Brick's face, the freckles, the brown eyes, the thick red hair falling over his forehead. How could she tell him? How could she ever say he couldn't go home?

She wrote it down carefully, the names of the lines, the bridges, the zigzags, even though she knew it was useless. Then she shut the map book in front of her and pushed back her chair.

Somehow she had to tell him.

16
Brick

He hated to leave that spot near that small bushy tree. He wished he knew what the tree was called. He reached up, pulled off a leaf washed by the rain, and put it in his pocket. Claude would know.

He looked across the park. The boy was still on the swing, going back and forth as if it were a sunny day. It was as if he didn't care about the rain pelting down on his head.

Mariel was there again without a sound. She sank down on the step, her head against the wall of the band shell, her hair flat and wet against her head. She closed her eyes. "Have to catch my breath."

He sat waiting; he could see the folded piece of paper in her hand. "You have it," he said.

She opened her eyes and looked down at the paper, too. "I have it," she said slowly. "But I was thinking. The rain will make it hard for you. Slippery . . ."

"The rain will make it easier," he said. "Not so hot walking. Don't worry." He wanted to tell her about the rain, how Mom loved watching it from their porch after supper. And when it stopped she'd listen to the crickets and katydids as they began their clicking and sawing again like strange instruments, in time for a moment, then out, then together again, thousands of them. "Stronger after the rain," she'd say, "like a summer orchestra."

Next to him Mariel's face was sad, her mouth drooping just a bit. She was sorry he was leaving. He felt it, too. After today he might never see her again.

He reached for the paper, sliding it through her fingers, feeling her pull against him a little. It was almost as if she didn't want to give it to him.

"Please . . . ," she began.

Something was wrong, worse than his leaving. He could see it in her eyes, and her fingers had begun that fluttering. "What is it, Mariel?"

She shook her head.

"Is it Ambrose?" he asked. "Something with Ambrose?" He wondered why he felt bad about Ambrose, why he hated to disappoint him by leaving. Claude would have liked Ambrose; Pop would have liked him, too. But then, thinking about it, he was sure of something. If Ambrose knew the story, the whole story, he'd understand. Ambrose would have done the same thing.

He opened the paper, looking at the map she had drawn, the directions in her small, even handwriting. "The bridge first," he read aloud.

She rubbed her hands against her dress. "It's a long walk to Windy Hill," she said. "You must have come farther in that car than we thought." She spoke slowly, looking away from him, the way Claude had the day he left. She stared at the center of the band shell. "Even to get to the Brooklyn Bridge is far."

"Which way is the bridge?"

She pointed over her shoulder.

He searched for the top of it in the distance, but all he could see were the trees in the park, huge trees against the gray sky.

"Far . . . ," Mariel said. "Even if you could walk ten miles a day . . ."

"I can walk farther than that. Much farther." He looked down at the paper, at the wavery lines she had drawn for roads, starting at one end of the page, trailing along the edge.

"Weeks," she said. "More than two hundred miles."

"I don't have weeks," he said.

Her fingers fluttered. She moved her hands down behind her back. "If only we had money, we could get you on a bus."

He stared at her for a moment, then turned away. He shoved the paper in his pocket and headed for the park entrance, going fast, faster as his feet hit the path.

Two hundred miles, a thousand miles? He had to get home.

17

Mariel

"Wait," she called, and went after him, tripping over their lunch bags, leaving them. She knew she couldn't catch up to him. Before she was halfway down the path, he went through the gate and ran along the sidewalk on the other side of the iron fence.

She went as far as the gate, still calling, but he was gone. She stood there in the rain, feeling it plaster her hair to her cheeks. She didn't know where to go. Not back into the park. Maybe she'd never go into the park again. But not to school either, not home, not even her chipmunk-safe room. She pushed her hair back. She had never felt worse.

"What about your stuff?" the other boy called.

"Our lunch bags? I don't want them."

"Can I keep them?"

She waved her hand over her shoulder. "Yes." She couldn't eat, couldn't imagine being hungry again.

Her legs were heavy, her limp worse than usual, and there was a sharp ache in her knees. She went outside the gate. Brick would be blocks away now, going in the direction of the bridge. She trailed her fingers along the black spikes around the park, seeing the boy just inside, opening one of the bags.

"Can I keep the book, too?" he yelled.

"Go ahead." She looked back. He held up a heavy book.

Claude's book?

"No," she called. "Not that."

"You said." His face was angry. "Finders keepers, anyway."

"Not the book." She said it in a Geraldine Ginty voice, a not-to-be-fooled-with voice. "Give it back or else."

"Or else what?" the boy began.

She couldn't think of what she'd do, but it would be something. No matter what, she was going to have that book. She started back into the park.

The boy rooted through the bag to see what else was inside. "Just the book," she said, "I don't care about the rest."

"All right," he said, his voice sullen. He tossed it to her. It landed on the wet grass and she scooped it up, rubbing it against her dress, drying it. She felt the thickness of it, the soft leather cover, saw the words in another language. What would Brick do when he realized it was gone?

She tucked it under her arm, trying to protect it from the rain; then she started for home, passing Ambrose on the street, his hat down over his eyes. He didn't even see her, although he could have. It was after school now, and kids were outside, jumping off stoops into puddles, sailing Popsicle sticks into sewer gratings. And luckily Ambrose turned the corner away from the bridge.

Mariel walked through the lot on the boulevard, its weedy smell strong in her nose, and moments later when she reached her own street, she didn't even remember how she had gotten there.

She went in the back door, stepping on the killer vines, silly game, and climbed the stairs. A picture of her mother came into her head. That red sweater, the bracelet dangling.

Her mother there in the middle of the night, but Mariel was too tired to open her eyes.

"Tomorrow, we'll have a wonderful surprise, Mariel, you'll see."

And in the morning, someone had lifted her out of the machine. It was a long round machine, easier to see now that she was on the outside instead of the inside. There was a hole in the top for her head, and a mirror so she could look around. But now the machine was turned off. No more whooshing. And she was in a chair, safe.

"Don't be afraid. See, you're breathing on your own. How does the world look?"

"Good," she had whispered, almost not making a sound, surprised there was no feeling against her chest, surprised that the machine wasn't breathing for her.

But everyone had heard her whisper. "Atta girl. Great girl . . . ," one of the nurses had said.

All those faces, and Loretta saying, "You see, you can do anything, Mariel."

And the ache in her knee now. She pressed it down with her hand as she stood at her chipmunk-safe bedroom door, looking at her everything table, her bed with the white chenille spread, and above the bed . . .

She leaned her head back against the door. *Above the bed . . .*

The two-dollar bet money.

"It's yours anyway," Loretta had said. "You can do anything."

She could take the money. She could find Brick.

And her mother, too?

She reached for the frame, lifting it gently off the hook, and went into the kitchen to rummage around in Loretta's junk drawer. She picked up the hammer.

It took only one good smash to break the glass, and then she turned the frame upside down over the garbage pail and shook it until the shards of glass were gone.

She knew time was going and finding Brick would be almost impossible. Loretta's words: *"Only one bobby pin in the whole house to hold on my cap. It'll be like finding a needle in a haystack."*

For another moment she stood there. *"You can do anything."*

She took the two-dollar bill with its gold seal out of the broken frame. She closed her eyes, touching it.

She reached for a pencil and a piece of paper on the table.

Dear Loretta. I've gone to find my mother. I have the two dollars. Brick and I will take the bus. I love you. Mariel.

She stood there for another minute thinking about Loretta. Loretta's hot temper. She picked up the pencil. *P.S. Throw a pot in the sink, but don't be angry with me!*

What else did she need? She pulled out cookies and peaches, slapped together two sandwiches, and dumped them on the table.

In her bedroom, she put on her straw hat with the daisies, snapping the elastic band under her chin, and pulled a sweater out of the drawer. She folded the money into her patent leather pocketbook, hurrying, going faster than she ever thought she was able to, and went back into the kitchen to stuff everything on the table into a bag with her sweater, and Claude's book wrapped in waxed paper. She pulled her umbrella from the stairs in the hall. She was ready.

She walked down the stairs, stepping on killer vines

all the way. Outside someone was listening to *Lorenzo Jones* on the radio. She stood there, trying to think, trying to plan.

It would take Billy Nightingale a long time to cross the bridge into Manhattan. It would take her forever. But somehow she had to be at the end of that bridge waiting for him as he crossed.

18

Mariel

*O*utside she pulled open the green-striped umbrella and started down Midwood Street. Suddenly she knew how she could catch up with Brick. The church bells tolled at six o'clock, and if she was at Jordan's candy store by then, everything might work out. *Might,* she told herself, crossing her fingers.

It all depended on Daisy, the ragman's horse.

Mariel turned the corner and stopped at Jordan's window, twirling her umbrella, looking at his display. Faded red, white, and blue crepe paper was bunched up around the edges of the glass; dead flies were scattered here and there. In the center was a shiny picture of Mr. Jordan himself in his army uniform from the Great War. Jordan was young in the picture, he had lots of dark curly hair, and best of all, he was shaking hands with President Wilson. Mariel could understand why he wanted that picture there, why he was so proud of it. She thought about the picture of President Roosevelt in his cape that Loretta had cut out of the newspaper for her, and Geraldine Ginty, hands on her hips. *"You're a liar, Mariel. There's no such thing as a President who can't walk."*

The six o'clock bells began to ring. Mariel looked up the street as a car went by and then another. Where was Benny? She leaned her head against the wet store window. Suppose he didn't come?

"The only thing we have to fear is fear itself" was what the President would say.

Inside, Jordan tapped on his counter with the edge of his ring. "Hey, Mariel, want to break the window?" He shook his head. "It's pouring rain. You kids are crazy."

She had always wanted to tell Jordan about President Roosevelt, but now wasn't the time. He looked hot and irritable. "Sorry," she said, and went to the edge of the sidewalk.

She leaned against the telephone pole, her package under one arm, holding the umbrella over her head with the other. After a while, the bell tolled again, once this time. It was six-thirty. What would she do if Benny didn't come?

She was about to give up when she heard Daisy's bells and Benny's voice. "Old rags, we buy, we sell."

Thank you, Daisy, she thought.

Benny pulled up in front of the candy store, his hat streaming rain. Jordan was at the window again, tapping with his ring, motioning to Mariel. "Want a sugar cube for the horse?" he asked. "Want one for yourself?"

She knew he was telling her he felt bad about the window business, so she smiled and put her package down. He reached around the door and handed them to her. "Good girl," he said.

Benny sat back as she held her hand out flat with both sugar cubes for Daisy to nuzzle. "It's the princess all dressed up," Benny said. "On your way to a party in the rain?"

"I need a favor, Benny," she said, looking at Daisy, afraid to look up, afraid he'd say no.

"Want an old rag? Want a dozen?"

"A ride, please."

"I'm not going very far," he said, grinning. "No castles on my route." He wiped his face with the back of his sleeve.

"I need to go to Manhattan."

His eyes widened. "That's far enough. What are you going to do there? Not running away, are you?" She saw him look down at her legs, biting his lip, sorry he had said that.

She picked up the bag. "I have to get this to a friend on Canal Street," she said, "but Loretta has to work."

All true, every bit of it.

He shook his head. "After Manhattan, I have to go to the Bronx. I'm doing extra time, extra money for my girl Gracie's birthday present." He hesitated. "That's a long way. Are you sure Loretta wouldn't mind?"

Mariel smiled. "Loretta says I can do anything. Besides . . ." She pulled at the elastic under her chin. "I don't need to come back. My friend . . ." She let her voice trail off, let him think she had a ride.

"All right then," he said. "I could drop you near the bridge. Know where that is?"

"Sure." She had never seen anything more than the top of it poked up when she went shopping with Loretta.

Benny held out his hand, fingers hard, palms calloused, and pulled her up next to him. They began to move, the old clothes shifting in back of them, the sleigh bells jingling, and Daisy trotting along in the puddles.

Mariel wondered if she'd really find Brick. Was she making a mistake going to the far end of the bridge? Should she wait on the Brooklyn side instead? She thought about it. It was a long bridge, she remembered that. If Brick started across before she got there, she'd miss him. She hated to think about that, waiting at the bridge all night, never seeing him, wondering what to do.

She closed her eyes and listened to Benny click his tongue against his teeth to spur Daisy on. He began to sing then, "Daisy, Daisy, I'm half crazy, all for the love of you . . ."

After a minute, she began to hum with him. Daisy went faster now, and they turned down a cobblestone street with the wagon rocking from side to side. "Daisy moves right along when she thinks she's going home," Benny said. "She has her own way of getting to the bridge."

Mariel nodded, holding on to the seat with both hands. Wouldn't it be wonderful if she found Brick? Wouldn't he be surprised?

19
___

Brick

He had found it. After circling blocks, going past the same vegetable store more than once, he glanced up to see the sign in front of him. FLATBUSH AVENUE!

He looked down at the paper: *Take Flatbush Avenue all the way to the bridge and cross into Manhattan.*

Easy directions, a long walk in the pouring rain. At first he jogged along the street, not minding it. He even stopped for a moment to watch the cars. He had seen more cars in the last few days than he had in his whole life: Model A Fords, and even a Packard or two.

He'd tell Claude all about them when he got there. He felt a quick stab of pain in his chest. Mariel had to be wrong about how long it would take. If only she were wrong! Giant buildings appeared in the distance, hazy against the clouds, the buildings of Manhattan, he was sure. But after walking blocks, they didn't seem closer.

He began to listen to the sound of his footsteps. The wet sidewalk was so much harder than the packed dirt of the Windy Hill road. He couldn't stop thinking of the cement against his feet. His sock kept pulling down inside his right shoe, rubbing against the skin of his heel. He was going to have a blister soon, and how could he walk all those miles with a sore foot?

He stopped in front of a barber shop, closed now, and slid down against the slippery red-and-white pole. He took off his shoes and tied them together to hang around his neck, then rolled up his socks, one for each shoe.

The street in front of him was filthy with torn-up papers, broken bottles, even a squashed box that some kids had made into a house for themselves, everything sopping wet. He'd have to be careful not to step on something sharp.

He stood up then, thinking to reach down for Claude's book, but it wasn't there.

Claude's book gone?

He sank down again, hunched over, his head bent. What had happened to it? Where had he had it last? He remembered having it in the park, sitting under that bushy little tree. He reached into his pocket to feel the softness of the leaf. How could he ever tell Claude?

"Something the matter?" A woman stood in front of

him, her hair tied up in a babushka, her face lined. She held a newspaper over her head for an umbrella.

He shook his head. "Just . . . ," he began, rubbing his chest, feeling the pain of losing the book.

"Too much candy," she said, making a shhh-shhh sound with her tongue. "Too much to eat. It will go away."

He nodded, then stood up with his shoes over his shoulder and moved away from her. How far to the bridge? Too far. Too many blocks barefooted. Not a cent in his pocket. No food. Certainly no food today, not until he got into the country and there'd be fruit on the trees and fields of vegetables. How long? He needed the taste of water in his mouth, on his tongue, in his throat. An orange soda, a root beer, cold and frosty. He held up his face, his mouth open to catch the drops of water.

Feeling sorry for himself, that was what it was. What would Pop say? He straightened up, walking on the outside edges of the soles of his feet. He could turn around, ask anyone where the nearest station house was, ask for Ambrose the cop, and he'd be back in the house on Midwood Street in time for supper.

But he wasn't going to do that. He had to put one foot in front of the other, step by step. He wasn't going to think about eating, or his feet. This was just the beginning of the trip.

The sidewalk was divided into cement blocks. He'd count to fifty and then another fifty, and then another.

Sooner or later, all those blocks of cement would get him to the bridge.

He wouldn't let himself think about what would happen after that, unless it was to picture himself sitting in Julia's kitchen, telling her and Claude about the long walk, telling them about Brooklyn.

After a while he noticed that it wasn't raining so hard; now there was only a soft drizzle. Windows opened along the avenue, and he could hear people's radios as he walked: the news, war in Europe, the Dodgers game in Chicago called because of rain.

It was getting dark. Lights came on in the houses, and in the backs of stores, and he was alone, hobbling down the street in the dark, his breath sounding loud in his ears. There was something he was beginning to realize. He would never be able to walk two hundred miles, not in time for the harvest, not unless he hitched a ride, or sneaked up into the back of a truck on its way to the country.

But suddenly, out of nowhere, he saw the lights of the bridge. They curved up over the span in front of him, a tall bridge with a few cars going back and forth.

Just get to the other side, he thought, *just get that far.* He would have done something then, gotten somewhere. He went up on the footpath and looked down into the shimmering black of the water below. He walked more quickly now. No one else was on the path in front of him.

In the traffic lane going toward Manhattan, a car went by, its wheels splashing water against the metal floor of the bridge. Its headlights threw large blocks of light that zigzagged across the footpath and left patches of darkness between the stanchions. As the car crossed the bridge in front of him, its lights lit up the end of the footpath. In the sudden gleam he noticed someone down at the other end, leaning against the railing under the light, a green-striped umbrella over his head.

He told himself it wasn't that far to the end, all he had to do was count the steps to that person and he'd be off the bridge, there on Canal Street.

He was halfway across and the person hadn't moved. He saw then that it was a girl. Under the umbrella she looked as if she were going to a party with her straw hat and a dress with a sash, and a purse looped over her arm.

He stopped because the girl looked so much like Mariel that he didn't want to go close enough to see it was a stranger. Mariel, who had become his best friend in just two days. And then he heard her call. "Billy . . . Billy Nightingale . . ."

He began to run toward her, seeing her smile as he came closer. He watched her pull Claude's book out of a bag and hold it in the air.

20

Mariel

The Canal Street subway had two sets of stairs to the trains. So many steps! She took them slowly, but still no one would believe she had done this, she thought as she dropped a nickel into the turnstile. No one but Loretta. *"You can do anything, Mariel. I really believe that."*

Loretta would be home by now, dropping her cap on the kitchen table, calling them. *"How about some root beer and a couple of cookies while we listen to the radio?"*

How would Loretta feel? she wondered.

And what about Ambrose the cop? Would he be angry when he found out she had run away? *Run home?* she thought. Strange, she had never seen Ambrose angry. He just showed up when he caught her playing hookey, and walked her back to school. It was like a game. The truth was, she thought in surprise, she liked Ambrose almost more than anyone she knew.

Now she and Brick rocked along in a subway train, and her two-dollar bill was gone, changed into coins by the ticket seller, stuffed into the cash register like all the other money people used.

The two-dollar bill! She'd never see it again. Would that make Loretta sad? As sad as Mariel felt? She opened her purse to feel the change the bill had made, all of it there except for the two nickels she and Brick had used for the subway.

She watched the stations flash by; they were headed for midtown Manhattan and the Shortline bus, Brick reaching into the bag of food for another sandwich, another piece of fruit.

She thought of Loretta again: *"I'd never been out of Brooklyn, but I had no family, and it was an adventure. There I was with my friend Mimi, both of us new nurses, on the eight o'clock Shortline to Windy Hill. I didn't even know I was on the way to you."*

"We won't be there until the middle of the night," Mariel told Brick, holding on to the strap and shouting over the noise of the train.

"We?" Brick asked. "We?"

She patted her patent leather pocketbook. "I have enough money for us both, and a tiny little bit left over just in case."

"We?"

"I'm going with you."

He didn't look as happy as she thought he might, he looked worried.

"What will Loretta say?" he asked. "What will Ambrose say?" But after a moment he grinned at her. "I know what Julia will say. She'll be glad to see you and so will Claude."

Mariel let out her breath with a whoosh. She smiled back and then she watched the train slide into Forty-second Street, and pulled him out the door with her.

They went up another set of stairs, slowly now. She didn't have enough breath to answer the questions he kept asking about what Loretta would say. And why would she want to go all the way to Windy Hill, anyway?

She couldn't pay attention to the questions. The next part was tricky, getting them from the subway to the bus terminal. But then she remembered.

The movie was Dumbo. *She and Loretta had sat in the balcony eating popcorn and peanut chews. They passed the terminal on the way back to the subway.*

"Poor elephant with his big ears," she had said.

Loretta grinned. "But didn't he do just fine?"

The lights in the bus terminal were far apart; there weren't enough of them to brighten the huge room; the exhaust from the buses hung in the air, thick in Mariel's nose and throat. But she was so glad to be there, she didn't care. It seemed, though, as if it must be the middle of the night, even though it wasn't even time to listen to *The Cisco Kid.*

The ticket seller looked doubtful as she slid the money toward him. "We're visiting our grandmother," Mariel said, snapping the elastic band under her chin.

He hesitated.

"You were a good brother to take me," Mariel said, trying to sound as if Brick were almost grown-up, trying not to look at him because they'd both laugh.

The man punched out two tickets, and they climbed onto the bus, sitting back against the smooth brown leather seats. Mariel sat at the window side, leaning against the pane as they pulled out of the terminal. The streetlights made the buildings around them hazy, but it had stopped raining at last.

She wanted to tell Brick why she was really there. Her fingers began that bit of trembling. She tightened them against the paper bag with the pieces of fruit that were left. "I had to bring you Claude's book," she began. "I knew you had to have it."

He nodded. "I'm really glad."

She shook her head. "But there's something else. I think I lived in Windy Hill once," she said. "Before Good Samaritan."

"On a farm? In the town?"

"I don't know yet."

"The room with the green lace curtains is there?"

"I don't even know that." She looked down at her hands clutching the bag, still now as she began. "It starts with the ambulance. No one remembers anything else. And I was only four."

"Someone has to remember," he said.

"Loretta tried to find out." She lifted her shoulders. "But there were so many kids with polio, and there were no records about me. Only the date I came, September third, 1934, and a torn piece of paper that said 'Mariel . . .' "

Her voice trailed off. Even the paper was gone by the time they had left the hospital. *Loretta had shaken her head. "Try to understand, honey. The hospital rooms were filled, the halls jammed with beds, and the nurses running around, working day and night. No time to bother with papers, no time for anything."*

Mariel sighed. She could see that Brick wanted to hear more, but there was such a little bit to tell: *Green lace curtains, when the wind blows . . . red sweater and a gold bracelet.*

He was thinking about it, feeling sorry for her, but it wasn't the way Frankie McHugh felt sorry. It was different, somehow, all right for him to look that way. "I'll help," he said.

"I know that," she told him.

They sat there, feeling the motion of the bus, and she told him about Benny the ragman, and Daisy in her straw hat, and perching up on top of the wagon, and then she saw that his eyes were drooping, closing, and he was asleep. But she was still wide awake, that feeling of excitement in her throat and chest.

She pressed her nose against the window as the lights cast an orange glow on the factories they passed, and then rows of stores. She wondered what Loretta was doing. A window was open next to the empty seat in front of her, and the air felt cool on her arms, almost too cool now. She squinted and the lights ran together in a line; she felt herself shiver.

"I like to be cold," she had told Loretta. The steaming packs Loretta plastered to the useless muscles of her legs were blistering hot. "I'd like to be in a blizzard, in a mountain of snow." She was angry. "If my mother was here . . ."

"There's a nurse from Australia named Sister Kenny," Loretta said. "She taught the world to loosen up these muscles with heat. Before that, legs stayed stiff and had to be braced." Loretta reached for another hot pack. "But you'll walk right out of here, Mariel."

Mariel closed her eyes, hugging herself for warmth, thinking of Geraldine Ginty and what she'd say if she found out Mariel was on a bus in Manhattan, New York.

21

Mariel

The dark wasn't Brooklyn dark with the streetlight glowing at the end of Midwood Street. Here in Windy Hill only one small light brightened the tiny station. Past that was nothing she could see. The noise of the crickets was loud, reminding Mariel that all kinds of living things were between her and the safety of Claude's house.

Even the driver seemed uneasy as he opened the doors. "No one's here to meet you?" he asked. "Maybe . . ."

But Brick was out the door before the driver could finish.

Mariel had to take the two steps more slowly. "Wait a minute," the driver said.

Mariel glanced back at him. She pretended she threw herself into horrible dark places every day. "Don't worry," she said. "We're fine. The house is just up the road."

If only the house really were just up the road.

And then she was off the step with Brick looking as uneasy as the driver had.

"Don't worry, Billy Nightingale," she said. "I can walk."

"It's a long walk."

She swallowed. "I can do it."

"Maybe you should wait. Claude has a little cart in his barn. I could come back for you."

Her eyes were getting used to the dark now. But stay here alone with the sound of a thousand insects ringing in her ears and strange rustling noises that might be anything? Never. Even the damp air smelled different, like cut grass maybe. "I can walk," she said again firmly, wishing she believed it. "I can walk almost as well as you can."

He took her hand as they started up the road. His hand had calluses that reminded her just a bit of Benny's. It was a good hand to hold, she thought. And as she looked up, she saw the stars, pinpricks of light flickering above her, and suddenly a sliver of a moon appeared, high and white, lighting the fields in front of her. She stopped, pointing up with the hand holding Brick's. "We never see all those stars in Brooklyn," she said. "Never."

He didn't let go of her hand. "Orion's Belt," he said. "Those three stars. And the Big Dipper with the North Star pointing the way."

"Even to Claude's," she said.

"Especially to Claude's." She could hear the catch in his voice. "And to my house just past that."

Suppose she found her mother? There was something she didn't want to think about. Why hadn't her mother looked for her?

She thought about Loretta then. Being without Loretta was terrible. At home her chipmunk-safe bedroom was empty. Loretta had come up the stairs from work, dropping her pointy nurse's cap on the table, and started dinner, and then . . .

Then . . .

"You're all I need, Mariel, to make me happy." Loretta *ran her hand over Mariel's head, and then she laughed. "It would be nice if we could find a guy, though, a husband for me, a father for you. But even so, we're a great pair just as we are."*

Loretta would have nobody.

She shook her head. She knew Loretta would be proud of her. *You can do anything.*

What Mariel wanted to do then was wait in the station, wait for the next bus and go right back to Brooklyn, to Loretta.

The road seemed to go on forever, up one hill, down the next, turning so that as she looked back even the glimmer of light at the station was gone. Rows of trees threw giant shadows across the fields. Were they apple trees like hers? And then the road turned again one last time. She saw lights through the trees, squares of light, yellow and warm, and heard a dog barking.

"It's Regal, Claude's dog," Brick said, and whistled.

Another moment and a light went on over the porch. A woman stood there, a small woman with a knot of hair on top of her head and a shawl thrown over her shoulders. She peered into the darkness, her hand on the dog's head. The dog stayed at her side only for a moment, then loped toward them, his tail wagging, circling around them, whining.

Brick let go of her hand, and crouched down, his arms going around the dog's neck. "It's me, Julia," he called.

He turned back to Mariel. "I'm home, Mariel," he said. "Home."

22
Brick

Everything was just the same in Julia's kitchen, even the pot of water on the stove. "Tea," she said, bustling around, not asking if they were hungry. She put thick wedges of bread on the table and a bowl of blackberry jam.

She hadn't asked about Mariel, not yet, but he knew she was wondering. And she wouldn't ask, not with Mariel looking tired enough to fall asleep at the table, but sitting up straight and stiff, her eyes anxious, her fingers moving against the blue-and-white tablecloth.

Brick looked up at the stairs, waiting to hear Claude come down with his heavy step, waiting to see Claude's eyes light up when he saw who was there. *"Thought I'd come in time for the harvest,"* Brick would say. He felt as if he couldn't wait one more minute.

Then he saw Claude's feet in the old work shoes on the steps, Claude's hands still bandaged, one of them touching the banister lightly, Claude's face. He couldn't say a word. He met Claude at the bottom of the stairs and Claude's arms went around him. Claude smelled of apples and the kitchen woodstove. They stood there for a long time, and still he couldn't say a word.

"I have been waiting for you," Claude said at last in his loud voice.

"That's true," Julia said, reaching up to tuck a strand of hair into her bun. "I told him he was a foolish old man, but he knew you were coming." She motioned to the table as she poured tea and then honey into mugs.

And now Claude saw Mariel.

She looked up at him, Brick thought, as if she knew she shouldn't be in Julia's kitchen, as if he might send her back out to the bus station again.

But Claude held up his bandaged hand. "Tell me," he said. "Are you the angel who brought Brick back to Windy Hill?"

She laughed and reached up to pull her elastic hat band over her head. She put her hat on the counter in back of her and reached for a piece of Julia's bread. "May I stay?" she asked.

Claude was smiling, too. "You've come a long way," he said. "And your family must be wondering."

She nodded uncertainly. "My family, Loretta, knows

I'm with Brick. She knows I was coming to Windy Hill. I left a note."

"All right then," Claude said. "This is what we will do. Tomorrow morning as soon as it is light—"

"Please," Mariel said.

"She has to stay," Brick said at the same time.

"Early tomorrow," Claude said, "you will go to the town and use the telephone at the post office." He looked at Mariel. "Is there a phone in your big city?"

"Jordan's," she said. "At the candy store."

Julia nodded, her gnarled hands around the teapot, warming them. "Yes, we will have to let them know, all of them, Brick's family, too." She turned to Mariel. "Sometimes Claude makes sense. Not too often, but on occasion." She frowned. "But what about school?"

Claude shrugged. "There is always time for school, but not just now." He took a noisy sip of his tea.

"The apples," Brick said. "The harvest."

Claude bent his head. "We have hung on for so long," he said. "Through floods and dry spells, but this time there is no saving us."

"I'm here to pick," Brick said. "You know that, Claude."

"But you are the only one," Claude said. "My hands are useless."

"Joseph and I—" Brick began.

"Joseph is old," Claude said. "Older than I. He says he's too old to climb. I think he has no heart left for it."

"Shhh." Julia's eyes glistened. "We will talk about this tomorrow. It is late, and you are tired."

Brick could hear Mom's voice in his head: *"It will look better in the morning,"* she'd say. *"It always does."*

But Claude was right. There was no way one person could pick the apples.

23

Brick

Outside the window, the barn and the trees were smudges of charcoal in the early-morning darkness. Brick thought he must be the first one awake. But Julia was in the kitchen, sitting at the same spot as if she hadn't moved all night, though she wore a flowered housedress and her bun was small and tight against the back of her head.

"I will make you breakfast," she said.

"Let me go outside first," he said. "I want to see the trees." He didn't want to tell her it was his house he wanted to see. He wanted to put his feet on the porch that ran around the front, take the key that was always hidden under the flowerpot, and open the kitchen door.

He wanted to touch Mom's yellow movie dishes on the shelf and go up the stairs to his own bedroom.

Julia pushed back her chair as if she'd go with him. "Even though it was such a dry summer," she said, "and even with the fire, the apples held on. It's hard to understand that now they will fall off the trees in their own time. Too late for us." She tried to smile. "Good for the deer."

What could he say to her? "I'll come back before Claude gets up."

She made a soft clucking noise. "That old man gets up later every morning. It's his hands. He feels helpless. For the first time, he is afraid."

Claude afraid. Brick thought of Claude in the orchard, his hands huge as he cut into an apple, showing him the seeds, running his knife along the center.

Brick could see it on Julia's face. She was afraid, too. Without the harvest money, they'd never be able to stay. And where could they go?

He went outside and walked along the wide path that separated one row of apple trees from another. A rim of pink at the edge of the sky shone through the trees to the east. He could see the damage the fire had done. On some trees the bark was stained black; on others, the leaves seemed sparse. But the apples were large, and in the early light, he could see they had turned a rosy color.

He put his hand on one of the trees, looking up. It was time to pick; just a twist and the apples would fall into his hands. He'd slide them into the bag he'd have slung over his shoulder and around his waist.

The path veered now; it wasn't as straight as it seemed. He turned, taking the narrow way to the top of the hill and his house. He climbed the fence between Claude's orchard and the ruined cornfield and leaned against it, his eyes on the brown roof with the double chimney.

He was glad their own orchard was hidden beyond the house. He'd hate to look at the blackened stumps, the twisted shapes that would never grow apples, never even grow green leaves. Pop's words on the day they planted came into his head. *"We'll have a harvest. We'll never have to leave this house. We'll stay here forever."* He thought of Mom dancing, humming along with the radio music.

He heard the uneven step and turned. Mariel was coming up to the fence she couldn't climb. She still wore the same dress, and she hadn't combed her hair yet. But she was wide awake even this early.

"There's a gate," he said, "halfway down." They walked together, one on each side of the fence, until he opened the rusted iron gate for her and they crossed the field to his house.

He wanted to run now, he was so anxious to feel the kitchen doorknob under his hand, but he waited for her.

"Go ahead," she said, waving her hand. "I know you're in a hurry. I'll catch up."

He shook his head and made himself walk slowly,

thinking of her waiting at the end of the bridge for him in her straw hat with the elastic band. He'd never forget it.

And then they were in the living room. It had a closed-up, unused feeling, and there were dead flies on the sill the way he had pictured them when he left. "I'll open a window," he said, banging on the sash to ease it up.

He pulled out the movie dishes to show her, and with the air blowing in the open window the room began to feel the way it usually did. Mom would have had a vase of daisies on the table, and maybe a bowl of apples, but even so, it was almost as if he hadn't been away at all.

It seemed as if Mom would be coming down the stairs to start breakfast, and Pop trudging in from the barn, kicking the mud off his shoes against the step.

Mariel watched him, her head turned to one side.

"What?" he asked.

"I was wondering what you were thinking."

He grinned at her. "Wondering where your hat is this morning. Wondering if that band under your chin hurts. Wondering . . ."

"The hat's on the dresser. I'll let you try it on, snap the elastic, see what you think."

He smiled, picturing a straw hat on his head, then led her outside again onto the porch. Their feet were loud on the board floor, and he stopped to watch the rocker with the broken leg moving gently in the wind that had come up.

Mariel caught her breath as she saw Claude's orchard spread out in front of them. "Lovely," she said.

He thought so, too. It was the most beautiful thing he had ever seen.

"I'm going to pick," Mariel said. She looked fierce.

"We have to put ladders under the trees," he said, not wanting to tell her how hard it would be. "We have to climb up to get most of them, and reach out to . . ."

". . . pull off the apples," she said.

"Right."

She went to sit on the rocker.

"Wait!" he said, but a moment later, she was sprawled on the porch floor, looking horrified as the chair lay collapsed under her.

He let her worry for a moment, holding in the laughter, before he told her. "That happens at least once a week. We have to put the whole thing together again."

She rubbed her elbow, looking up at him. "Loretta says I can do anything."

He looked at her uncertainly.

"We're going to find out if she's right," she said.

He bit his lip. He and Mariel would be up in the trees, and Julia below with the baskets. Could they do it? "I'll tell you something, Mariel," he said. "If it can be done, we'll do it, you and I. We'll do the harvest, and find out about your mother." He swallowed. "We have to try."

He bent down then to knock the rocking chair back together. "Let's go to see Joseph. Maybe he'll help."

24

Mariel

*M*ariel stared at herself in Julia's mirror. Julia's shape-less dress actually looked nice on her, she thought. The skirt covered most of her knees, and the rosy color made her cheeks look pink.

Julia was outside waiting for them, and they went to town sitting in the back of her dusty pickup truck. Mariel looked carefully at the little main street, the feed store, the ice cream parlor, and then up at the hospital on the hill. She had expected to recognize something. *There, she'd say, that's where I got sick. . . . But before that . . .*

All of it was strange. Not a street, not a building seemed familiar to her.

Julia came inside with them. "I must talk to your parents," she said. "They must know that you're with me, that you're safe."

The phone was on the wall, waiting for them. And then, suddenly, Mariel couldn't wait to talk to Loretta, couldn't wait to tell her she had gotten herself all the way to Windy Hill. "All because of you," she'd tell Loretta. She caught her breath. Suppose Loretta was angry, really angry.

"Number, please," the operator said.

"In Brooklyn," Mariel said. "On Bedford Avenue. Jordan's candy store."

The phone rang in the dark booth in back of Jordan's store, seven, eight, ten times. Mariel remembered sitting at the counter one time, watching Jordan as he counted out change, never hurrying as the phone rang and rang.

At last he was there, sounding as if he were standing next to her.

"Please, could you get Loretta Manning for me?" she asked.

"Is it Mariel?" Jordan said. "Oh, Mariel. Stay there, girlie. Don't move." She could hear him calling to someone: "She's on the phone. It's all right. I think she's all right."

It took forever before Loretta picked up the phone. Mariel counted off in her mind: Jordan sending one of his kids along Bedford Avenue, turning into Midwood, up the block, ringing the bell.

Loretta's voice was breathless. "Mariel?" she said. "Is it you?"

Mariel could hardly talk. "Yes, it's me," she said.

"I ran all the way," Loretta said, "every step."

"I knew you would." Mariel pictured Loretta's hair flying, lipstick crooked. She held the phone tight to her ear.

"Are you all right?" Loretta began. "And is Brick with you?"

"Of course," Mariel said. "I want to help with the apple harvest."

"The apple harvest," Loretta said as if she couldn't believe it.

"And I want to find—"

"Where are you? Good grief, Mariel. Tell me right this minute."

Mariel blinked. "I'm in Windy Hill."

"It must be two hundred miles!"

"At Claude's farm."

"Claude," Loretta said.

"Brick's friend who has an orchard." *There must be something wrong with the phone,* she thought. Loretta kept repeating everything. "I told you in my note."

For a moment Loretta didn't answer. "A note?"

Mariel closed her eyes. The bag of food on the kitchen table. Scooping everything up: peaches, sandwiches. The note? Her hand went to her mouth. "Oh, Loretta, I'm sorry. I'm so sorry." She broke off. "Listen, maybe you shouldn't tell Ambrose I'm gone."

"What do you think? That I've been sitting around,

not looking for you?" Loretta stopped and then went on. "Do you think no one cares about you? The whole Seventieth Precinct is looking for you. And everyone you know. Benny, blaming himself. Jordan. Ambrose up all night."

Loretta really was angry. Mariel bit her lip.

"And Geraldine Ginty. On her roller skates, up and down early this morning, street after street, and Frankie McHugh searching through Prospect Park, even though Benny said you were in Manhattan. How could you do that?"

Looking for her. Everyone. She leaned back against the wall, trying to think of what to say. "I miss you so much, Loretta. It's terrible without you."

Loretta sighed. "Shall I come get you?"

"I think I can do this," Mariel said slowly.

Just as slowly, Loretta answered. "Mariel, there's nothing you can't do. I knew that from the first day in Good Samaritan."

"I want to find my mother."

She could hear the sound of Loretta's breath. "Oh, Mariel." She was silent. And then, "Now listen, I'd come up in a minute. I'd come and get you and take you home."

"But . . . ," Mariel began.

Loretta sighed. "You have to do this yourself. I know that."

"Don't be mad, Loretta."

"If you were here . . ."

"Would you throw me in the sink like the burned pot?"

Loretta laughed. "I love you, Mariel."

Mariel swallowed. "Julia, Claude's wife, wants to tell you everything's all right. She lent me her dress, and, oh, Loretta, I'm sorry you didn't know." She looked down at her fingers, tapping on the thick rubber of the phone cord.

"Will you send me a letter every day? Will you . . ." Loretta stopped. "We'll catch up with school when you're home."

"Ambrose. What will Ambrose say if I'm not in school?"

"Send Ambrose a letter, too."

They both laughed, and then Julia was on the phone, speaking in her high fast voice, saying, "I know, I know," over and over, and then the money dropped, and Loretta was gone.

Loretta was gone and she hadn't even told her about the two-dollar bill.

But then it was Brick's turn. She heard him say something, and then the muffled voice of his mother on the other end. She half listened as he said it was all right, that Loretta knew, and Claude knew, and as soon as it was all over, he'd study in school, study forever if she wanted him to. Mariel didn't listen to Julia talking next. All she could think of now was Loretta, and Ambrose, and even Geraldine Ginty looking for her.

They left the post office, Julia to shop, and Brick to show her the way to Joseph's old farm. It was easy to see the path the fire had taken. The fields to one side were black and ruined. A burned smell still hovered in the air. But the other side was untouched. Butterflies hovered over the tall grass, and stalks of pink gladioli marked off a small garden.

Joseph's house had been saved: a shack without paint or a chimney, with cracked windows and a rickety porch. Inside, the walls were papered with old newspaper, and the only furniture was a cot in one corner and a table near the door. Joseph sat there, whittling at a piece of wood with a pocketknife. "The Tiernan boy, isn't it?" He squinted at Mariel. "Know you, too?"

"My friend, Mariel," Brick said, leaning forward to look at the small figure of a dog Joseph was carving. "We've come about Claude's harvest."

Joseph raised one shoulder. "No harvest this year." He looked through the open door, across the field, his eyes dim. "The last orchard is going under."

"There are two of us," Brick said, talking through him. "Mariel and I. We're going to do it. We just need . . ."

Joseph's eyes narrowed as he glanced at Mariel. "Not with those legs."

She felt a quick flash of anger. "They're the only ones I've got." She straightened up. She had never said anything like that before, not to Geraldine Ginty, not to anyone.

Joseph's lips went back against his teeth; maybe it was his way of smiling. "Spunky," he told her, "but it won't help." He leaned forward. "Claude's old. I'm old. My eyes are going. Claude's hands . . ." He shook his head. "The heart went out of the pickers years ago. It's a hard-luck valley. Empty houses, empty barns." He ran his hand over the gray stubble on his cheeks. "What's the use?"

"I'm going to pick," Brick said. "Every apple on every tree, even if it's winter by the time I'm finished." He stood up and stamped across the room and down the wooden steps.

"Please," Mariel said, her hands together. "Please."

He shrugged, and looked down at his carving, blowing away the shavings. "Have to think about it."

She put her hand on the table. "We have to start soon," she said.

She backed away from him and went down the steps after Brick. When she looked over her shoulder, Joseph was still at the table, knife in his hand, turning the little dog over. It seemed as if he had forgotten about them already.

25

Mariel

$\mathcal{A}$t lunchtime, Mariel and Brick sat outside on the back steps. Julia had made sandwiches, slices of ham with cloves on homemade bread. *Loretta would have loved this*, Mariel thought, the hot mustard, the sour pickle, but she was too excited to eat.

Was that the word, *excited*?

No, she was afraid. She could feel her heartbeat in her throat and a wave of sickness in her stomach. Now that she was going to see the hospital, all she could think about was her chipmunk-safe bedroom and missing Loretta.

Julia's soft voice and the rumble of Claude's carried through the open kitchen window. The radio was playing Loretta's favorite song. There were no real words to it, just Glenn Miller's sweet music. Mariel closed her eyes, listening to it.

Then Claude must have turned the dial to the sports news. This weekend the Dodgers would play a double-header with Chicago to make up for the rainout. "They'll have to take those games if they want to win the pennant," Claude told Julia over the voice of the announcer.

Next to Mariel, Brick wiped a streak of mustard off his finger. "It's a long walk to the hospital," he said, "but I know a shortcut through the trees."

She had pictured herself going alone; she wanted to go alone. She bit her lip trying to think of how she could tell him. But he seemed to know. "I'll just show you where it is," he said.

She nodded, relieved, then finished her sandwich slowly, brushing the crumbs off Julia's dress. And then they went up over the hill, and through the trees around Brick's farm, Regal, the dog, plodding along with them. She wondered what she was going to find at the hospital. She closed her eyes, then stumbled, reaching out to save herself against one of the trees. Something, she told herself. There'd be something there to remind her, or someone. Her mother had been there, leaning over her, she knew that, and she'd remember her face, or her name.

Maybe she'd remember.

It was a long walk, so long that she thought she'd have to give up, but then the trees thinned and the chimneys of the hospital stood tall and dark across the road in front of them.

Brick pointed, then slid down against one of the trees. "I'll wait here."

She went down the hill, trying to put one foot in front of the other as evenly as she could in case he was watching. And he must have been. "I hope . . . ," he called after her, without finishing.

She didn't turn but raised her hand to wave back before she crossed the road. There in front was the hospital sign with the large red-and-blue cross. Her feet crunched against the gravel, and she heard the sound of the fountain splashing even before she saw it. She stopped in front of the statue of the Good Samaritan with his kind face and outstretched hands.

Rolling along the gravel path in the borrowed car that would take them to Brooklyn, Loretta smiling: "Let's get out for a minute. I want to take your picture: Mariel Manning standing on her feet." In the hospital for two years. Not four years old, almost six now. And winter, not summer. Smelling the cold, raising her fingers to touch the swirling snowflakes . . .

Winter, not summer.

Her hand went up to her mouth. *Green lace curtains, fine day.*

A summer day. It had happened in the summer.

She shook her head. She knew that, she had known it all along. But she'd never thought about it before. Summer.

She took the path, then pushed open the heavy glass doors. Inside, the halls were just as shiny, the doors wide for wheelchairs, and she stood there waiting for a picture of her mother to come into her head. Instead she thought of Loretta, cap on crooked, cape flying, as she dashed down the hall.

The stairs were in front of Mariel now, and she climbed them, holding on to the railing. The huge room with iron lungs, maybe ten of them almost back to back, would be near the center of the hall. Hers had been near the window, a monster made of metal, a black cocoon so big that only her head stuck out as air pressed down on her lungs and forced her to breathe with that soft whoosh of a sound. And all she could see was reflected in the small mirror in front of her: a bit of green outside the window, the tan wall, and Loretta leaning over her. One other thing: a paper doll, Betty Boop with red cheeks and a bow mouth, pasted up on the edge of the mirror. *"A friend to talk to when I'm working,"* Loretta *had said.*

Funny, Mariel thought, she hadn't remembered Betty Boop in all this time, not Betty, nor the bit of green in the mirror.

She reached the top step and went down the hall slowly, touching the bricks, the guardrail, remembering how hard she had held it, and the first time she was able to walk alone, holding her hands in the air, showing Loretta she didn't need it anymore.

A nurse appeared in front of her now, and Mariel smiled at her. But the nurse frowned, her face irritable. "You're not supposed to be up here."

Mariel swallowed. "I was here," she said.

"There are sick people here, some of them contagious." The nurse shook her head.

"I need to see it again," Mariel said. "I'm looking for—"

The nurse put her hands on her hips. "If you're looking for someone, you have to go to the office and get a pass." She waved her hand. "That's all I need," she muttered, "kids wandering around."

Mariel didn't move. She reached out to touch the bricks again with one finger. But the nurse took a step toward her. "There are guards, you know. I'll have to call one of them."

Mariel felt a burning in her throat, her hands tapping against Julia's pink dress. She looked over her shoulder at the door to the room with the iron lungs. She could even hear the soft whooshing of the machines.

"You don't belong here," the nurse said, following her as she went toward the stairs, and stood at the top step until Mariel reached the hallway on the first floor.

Outside she leaned against the door, the sun in her eyes, sound of the fountain in her ears.

There was nothing of her mother here. After all those years of thinking about her, wondering about her, dreaming of her! She had been so sure. Loretta would say Mariel didn't belong there in the hospital either, hadn't belonged there for a long time.

Brick had crossed the road. He was coming toward her. How lucky he was, she thought. He knew where he belonged.

26

Brick

He didn't ask; he didn't have to. Mariel hadn't found what she was looking for. She'd been inside only a few minutes. She followed him back to Claude's orchard without a word.

He tried to fill up the silence, tried to talk about anything except the hospital and her mother. "You can get up on a ladder," he said. "Both of us can do that. Julia will fill the baskets underneath. We'll get a start." He tried to smile. "We'll eat apples as we go along."

She stopped and leaned her head against a tree.

"Mariel?"

"I know," she said. "I'll help. I just have to get used to this."

"Want to tell me?"

She shook her head. "Nothing. Nothing happened. Everything is just the same."

They walked back through the trees toward Claude's house. He couldn't wait to get into Julia's kitchen. She'd see that something was wrong and somehow help him to make Mariel feel better. At least there'd be talking and not this terrible quiet with only the soft sound of their footsteps on the path.

But when they opened the kitchen door, Julia's back was toward them. She was bent over the table, a rolling pin in her floury hands, smoothing out circles for pies.

Brick went around the table, hoping she'd turn and see Mariel's face, but instead she thumped with the rolling pin, saying, "Root beer or tea in the icebox. It's so hot outside you must be thirsty."

At least it wasn't quiet in the kitchen. The radio blared from the windowsill and Claude creaked back and forth in his rocking chair, his laced-up shoes hitting the floor each time he came forward. He shook his head when he saw them. "No pennant for the Dodgers this year, I think. They've just lost the game in Chicago, five to four. And, just as bad, St. Louis won theirs. They've pulled ahead of the Dodgers."

Brick opened the icebox and pulled out two bottles of soda. He began to pour, watching Mariel from the corner of his eye. She was staring out the window. "They'll lose tonight's game, too," she said. "And St. Louis will win theirs."

"Maybe not." He picked up one of the glasses; it was

cool and wet in his hand. He put it on the table next to her, but she didn't even look at it.

"Loretta was counting on them," Mariel said.

From the rocking chair, Brick saw Claude glance across at her, his thick eyebrows raised. "When we first came here," he said in his rumbling voice, "Julia and I thought we'd never get started, but we did."

Julia turned now, a spot of flour on her cheek. "It's not the starting that's so hard," she said. "It's the finishing up."

But Claude had changed his mind about the Dodgers. "They'll come back, you'll see. Once you begin, you can't let it go."

"Do you think so?" Mariel asked.

"I think so." He smiled at Julia's back. "The Dodgers will win, we'll make the harvest. . . ." He raised one shoulder. "At least we'll begin first thing in the morning."

That night they sat up late around the kitchen table, finishing the pie Julia had made, the pitcher of iced tea empty, their dinner plates soaking in the sink. Insects hit the porch light with a pinging sound, and the Dodgers lost again, the score even worse: five to two. And when Red Barber announced that the St. Louis Cardinals had just won their game, Claude stood up and switched off the radio.

27
Brick

They were up early the next morning. Brick waited for Mariel; then they took out a few of the sacks that Julia had laid out. "Last year I raced with my father to see who'd fill the first sack," he told her. "He won, but just, and I would have beaten him this year, I think."

The trees were broad and low with branches pruned so each one had its space in the sun. He set one of the ladders against a tree for her. How pretty she was, even when her face was sad. He wondered if she knew that. He wondered how much she minded about her legs.

Julia came out of the barn, waving, with Claude in back of her, his old straw hat jammed down on his head. They dumped piles of bushel baskets into the back of the pickup truck, Claude using his wrists to balance them, then drove as close to the trees as they could get. By the time Brick filled his first sack, the baskets were in place under the trees along the rows.

He had dreamed about this harvest all winter, the smell of the apples, and the sound of the bees, and the blue September sky. But this was all wrong. Last year there had been enough of them with Claude, Pop and Mom, and Julia filling the baskets with Joseph. But this year the long rows of trees seemed endless.

"I'm going to earn my keep," he told Claude as Claude came down the row toward him.

Claude nodded, smiling. "I know that," he said. "I always knew it. And when you're finished, there's something else I must ask you to do."

"Anything," Brick said.

"The fence needs fixing. I've thought about it since the fire. But first the apples, yes?"

Brick nodded. As he talked with Claude, he watched Mariel uneasily. He didn't want to tell her to be careful. When she climbed, she'd have to hold on to the ladder or a branch with one hand to steady herself and reach for apples with the other. It would be awkward for her, slow. Could she do it? Claude and Julia wondered, too, he knew that. Julia pretended to be busy, unloading apples from the sack he held down to her, and Claude watched from in back of the ladder.

Mariel took the first step up, holding on with both hands, and then the second very slowly. Claude glanced at him, raising one shoulder the slightest bit. Mariel watched the ladder instead of the tree, and then the ground beneath her, and he wasn't sure she'd be able to reach for the apples.

But then she did reach out, her head still bent, groping. Her fingers closed around an apple, she pulled, and it was in her hand.

"Hey," Brick said. "The first one."

"That's good," Claude said in his gruff voice, and Julia clapped her hands. "Careful," she said.

Mariel glanced across at them, holding the apple like a trophy before she slid it into the bag that hung from her shoulder.

Her head went back then, and she looked up into the tree slowly, one foot on the third step, almost frozen there. She didn't move, she didn't reach out. He thought he heard her say something, but he could see only her back and her hands clenched on the rung above her, as she stared up at the branches.

He took another sack from Julia, feeling the coarse fabric under his arm, and heard the sound of her ladder falling.

He was down in a moment, his own ladder tipping as he went toward her. She was on the ground, her elbow and her knees skinned, rocking back and forth.

Julia and Claude reached her first, Julia patting her face, and Claude reaching out clumsily. "Are you all right, Mariel?" he asked.

Brick crouched down next to her, and she smiled at him, pointing up at the tree, holding her elbow with one hand. "It wasn't a green lace curtain. Never a curtain. It was always the leaves above me. Look, aren't they beautiful?"

He nodded, looking up, too, at the green against the blue sky. It was something he had seen often, the small leaves quiet on a cloudy day, or trembling in a storm. And in winter, he'd watch the bare branches, anxious for the first bit of color that would appear in May.

Mariel scrambled up, her eyes still on the branches over her head. "And all the time I thought it was a room with a curtain."

"Come into the kitchen," Julia said. "You need a bandage, maybe a glass of cool water."

"It's nothing." She brushed at her dress. "I would have been too young to climb by myself," she said slowly. "Someone must have carried me up into the trees." She stopped, her knuckles up to her mouth. "My mother? Could it have been my mother . . ."

Brick finished for her. ". . . picking apples?"

They nodded at each other, as Julia rubbed one of her hands against the other. "We should never have let you go up on the ladder. I thought it was too much . . ."

"I can do it. Really I can." Mariel stopped, thinking, staring at the leaves, a few of them tipped with the yellow of fall. "A green lace curtain," she said, reaching out to touch the trunk of the tree. "I want to talk with Joseph again."

28

Mariel

*I*nside Joseph's little house everything was quiet. Mariel knocked, then pounded at the door. When he pulled it open suddenly, she stepped back, startled. "Sorry," she said.

"You're the one making all that noise? You don't look big enough for that."

"Will you tell me . . . ," she said, not knowing how to begin.

"I'll tell you to sit on the porch there," he said, "and I'll fix you a lemonade."

She shook her head. "You don't have to."

"I need it myself," he said.

She sat on the edge of the old chair waiting for him. Cobwebs were everywhere; a furry brown spider swung from one porch railing to another. She wasn't afraid of it; she had other things to think about.

She had been there, in one of the orchards in the valley, she was sure of it: her mother picking apples with baby Mariel slung over her shoulder. *When the wind blows, the cradle will rock, and down will come . . .*

Mary.

. . . down will come Mary, cradle and all.

Not Mariel? Mary?

Her heart began to pound against her ribs. The sound of it was so loud, she thought even Joseph might hear her in his kitchen.

Joseph, who might know something that might help her.

He came out, handing her a glass of lemonade. "Warm," he said. "No ice today."

She nodded. *I was here. I was Mary.* "Why don't the apple pickers come?"

He sipped at the warm drink, making a face. "I don't talk about that," he said at last.

She was so close to him, inches away. If she could just see into his head. Her hands fluttered, and her knees trembled under Julia's dress. "I had polio," she said. "I was in Good Samaritan Hospital."

He chewed at his lip. "Were you?"

"I think I was with the apple pickers."

He rocked back in his chair, raising the drink to his mouth, not speaking for so long that Mariel thought he wouldn't tell her.

And then he held up four fingers as if it were an effort. "I knew four of the pickers." He raised his shoulder. "At night they camped in tents along the river, and then all of a sudden they were sick, really sick, all in one night. Polio. First a teenager, then one of the men, and then a young woman named Mary . . ."

"And her little girl," Mariel guessed.

He sighed. "Everyone was terrified. How had it come? Who would be next? Mary died here. She never even got to the hospital."

Died. Her fingers went to her mouth. *But hadn't she really known that? Hadn't she always known that?*

He nodded. "They didn't want to touch the little girl. She was only four. They knew she was dying. Someone went for the telephone in town to call an ambulance. Someone else took a scrap of paper, pinned it to her so they'd know her name: Mary Elliot . . ."

Mariel . . .

"They heard the sirens and scattered. They never came back."

She had a name. She had a mother.

"I was with them," he said in a voice so low she could hardly hear him.

"You knew them," Mariel said. "Knew the mother, knew the little girl."

"I knew them all," he said. "I was too old to go with them afterward, too beaten down. There had been so much laughter and singing, and the little girl, always clinging to her mother, such a happy little girl. And then in a few hours it was over."

He took a sip of his drink. "Sometimes I see a few of them in the next valley." His face was wet with tears. "It was the beginning of bad luck. Polio, then the orchards going under, people leaving. The pickers never came back." He sighed. "I buried the mother myself in the corner of the field. No one ever knew. I stayed on here. The house was empty, not belonging to anyone."

In the corner of the field, the flowers were a patch of soft pink against the long grass. The glass of lemonade in Mariel's hand seemed too heavy to hold. She reached out and rested it on the railing near the little brown spider.

"You were that little girl then," Joseph said. "I can see it now, the eyes, the sandy hair." His eyes were old, faded blue, bloodshot. He blinked, looking at her. "Maybe you'll bring back our luck."

"She picked with me on her shoulder, recited nursery rhymes . . . ," Mariel began, and broke off. "Could you tell me anything else? Even what she looked like?"

He chewed at his lip, trying to remember for her, she knew that. She listened to the sound of the crickets in the field, a tiny part of it her mother's. She waited for him to tell her something, wanting to see the pictures of her mother that were in her head.

"She wore a blue kerchief and had a sweet face like yours," he said. "She wore old shoes with the laces knotted." He leaned forward and touched her arm, a feather of a touch. "She had no family. You were all she had. And I can tell you the only thing that really mattered . . ."

She knew what he was going to say before he said it.

"She loved you," he said. "She really loved you."

Mariel reached out to the railing and pulled herself up. She leaned over to kiss Joseph's whiskery cheek, then went down the steps and across the field. The grass was high and she could feel it brushing against her legs. It felt scratchy and strange, and there was a buzzing from hundreds of insects, crickets maybe, she thought, as she watched something small and green sail in a wide arc from one lacy wildflower to another.

She came close to the stalks of pink flowers. They stood like soldiers in front of her, and it wasn't until she was almost on top of them that she saw the masses of small yellow buds that covered the circle they surrounded.

She bent down and gently ran her hands over the tiny petals. "I had a mother," she said, her voice sounding strange in her ears. "I had a mother who loved me, and her name was Mary. And that is my name, too."

29
Brick

From the ladder, Brick could hear Red Barber's voice on the radio. Today the Dodgers were in St. Louis, playing the Cardinals, their biggest threat. He could smell tonight's dinner, too, beans and molasses, and corn bread in the oven.

It made him think of Mom's kitchen, empty with the windows closed on this fall day. If she had been home, braided coffee rings with fat raisins would be cooling on top of the stove, and the smell of coffee would be drifting out across the fields.

When Claude went into the barn for something, Brick stepped off the ladder and sank down on the ground to rest for a minute. His arms hurt from reaching up, and he rubbed the back of his neck.

He hadn't told Claude how upset Mom had been. *"What about Loretta? You just left her? And school? Oh, Brick."* He bit his lip. He hated it when Mom wasn't happy with him. But Pop was glad, he knew that. And he knew he had done the right thing. When he saw Mom, he'd make her see that.

He squinted down the even row of trees in front of him. He'd never finish, he knew that now. What he could do would be enough to keep Claude going for a little while, certainly not the whole winter. But he had done his best.

He took another breath and stood up, ready to go back up the ladder. The late-afternoon sun slanted through the trees. What was taking Mariel so long? It was a short walk to Joseph's, and the old man wasn't that friendly. He should have gone with her.

He walked to the road, but she was nowhere in sight. He thought about it, then called to Claude.

Claude came out of the barn, wire looped over his arm. "Little by little, I can feel the strength coming back into my hands."

Brick nodded. "I think I'd better look for Mariel," he said. "It's been hours."

"Yes. Go ahead," Claude said. "Do you want me to come with you?"

"No, I can go alone." He went through the orchard, climbed the fence, and took the shortcut around the back of his house. As he reached the road he saw her.

She stopped and stood there in the middle of the road.

He looked at her face carefully, trying to see what she was thinking. Her fine hair was blowing a bit, and her eyes were filled with tears, her cheeks wet with them. "I found out about my mother, Billy Nightingale," she said. "Her name was Mary. That's my name, too."

"Don't cry," he said. "Please don't cry."

"It's all right to cry for your mother," she said.

He nodded, thinking of Mom, and took her hand as they walked.

"Tomorrow," she began. She could hardly get the words out. "Tomorrow I think we'll have help." She waved her hand. "Joseph was getting out his old car. . . ."

"That awful rattletrap," he said, trying to make her smile.

"He told me it would get him to the next valley." She swiped at her cheek. "There are pickers who'll come, Joseph said, when he tells them the end of the story. He'll tell them that luck changes even in Windy Hill."

"The end of the story?"

"It will take me forever to tell you that," she said. "And I'm going to do it, but after I get up on a ladder and look at my green lace curtain, and pick apples the way my mother did."

30
Brick

It happened the way Mariel said it would. They heard it from the kitchen, at first light, the sound of a car coming up the road. The motor rattled, and as they looked out the window, Brick could see it: an old black Ford, covered with dust, missing the front fender, almost like Joseph's.

On each side of the car someone stood on the running board, and there were people in the backseat.

He grabbed one of Julia's warm rolls in his hand. He was the first one outside, ahead of Claude. Three of them were inside the car, two out, the women wearing bandanas, one of them with a baby slung over her shoulder.

They talked with Claude, his napkin still tucked in his shirt, bandages off his hands for the first time. Then one of the pickers brought a pile of bushel baskets from the barn; the mother put her baby under a tree on a plaid blanket. Someone was singing a song about apple blossoms.

They climbed, tossing apples to each other. And by the time Joseph arrived, looking pleased with himself, Julia had come outside to set up a table with coffee and rolls and juice in pitchers.

They picked all that day, even in the darkness as Claude lighted kerosene lanterns to give them an extra hour. They were back the next morning and again the next. Brick watched Mariel, climbing more easily now, stopping to eat an apple, juice running down her chin.

He heard her ask, but none of them remembered Mary. They had known about the year that polio had come to the valley, though, and the little girl who had been lost.

By lunchtime on the third day, bushel baskets towered with apples, and Julia was at the wheel of the pickup truck to make her first trip to the market. "It's a good harvest," Claude told the pickers gratefully, "even after the fire."

That afternoon they were gone, on their way to another farm, still singing.

Brick sat on the back step before supper, his eyes closed, his hand on Regal's head. He listened to a bee buzzing back and forth under the porch roof, and Mariel talking in the kitchen with Julia. He had never been so tired.

"Brick?"

He jumped. Claude, his hat pushed back, his forehead red with sunburn, stood over him. "One more job?" he asked.

Brick straightened. "I can try."

Claude leaned on the railing. "We'll need fence posts. I have them cut in the barn."

Repair the fence? He was so tired. He wondered how he could do it.

"It's too big a job for today. But I want to show you where it needs doing. Walk with me."

Brick stood up, stepping over Regal. They took the path under the trees that led toward his house. He wanted to say that he loved it there, but he was embarrassed to say it aloud even to Claude.

"You belong here," Claude said, his voice gruff, "not in Brooklyn."

Brick nodded. "I know."

"But the girl," Claude said, "little Mariel. Tough little girl, she's just finding out how tough and strong she is."

"She belongs in Brooklyn," Brick said.

"With Loretta and the Dodgers." Claude smiled. "She just needs to find it out for herself." He patted his pocket. "There's a letter here for her. I have to remember when we go up to the house."

Claude looked at him seriously. Brick knew what he

was going to say: *"You'll have to go back with her, but maybe next year . . ."*

Claude waved one hand. "You see the trees out there . . ."

The orchard was more yellow than green now and a few leaves were beginning to drift down along the rows.

"After Julia and I came from Normandy, we were really alone. We never had a son."

Brick felt that ache, wishing for Pop.

"But the night you arrived with Mariel," Claude said, "Julia and I stayed up talking about all that had happened to us, and how you saved the orchard."

Brick shook his head. It seemed so long ago now.

"We felt as if we had a grandson, as if we had a family. You, and your mom and dad, just over the hill. It was terrible when you left." He reached out and put his hand on Brick's shoulder. "We knew how hard it must have been for you to come all the way home."

"Mariel got us here," Brick said, thinking about her standing at the edge of the bridge in Manhattan in her party dress and straw hat, twirling her green-striped umbrella.

"But I want to talk to you about the trees. For now, we're going to fence off the section closest to your house." Claude patted his shoulder with his broad hand. "It's for you."

Brick began to shake his head. There were as many trees as he and Pop had planted together. A stand of trees large enough to be its own orchard. Rows of trees, straight and green, the marks on the trunks to remind them of this summer. "I can't . . . ," he began.

"You can," Claude said. "You will. What good is all this to us when we see your house empty and know what you've done for us? Stay here with us this winter and go to school. I know your parents will agree. And when they come back in the spring . . ."

"We'll never have to leave again." He wouldn't have to go back to Brooklyn. He could stay right there with Julia and Claude. Stay forever. He could see it all: Mom coming out on the porch, wiping her hands on her apron, listening to the cry of the barn swallows, the crows on the fence; Pop waving from the tractor as the dark earth turned up and over in back of him. There'd be rows of corn coming, tiny shoots of green; and apples, an orchard of apples, shiny and new.

They'd stand in a circle in the kitchen. . . .

"Claude." It was Julia's voice.

"She wants me to eat something," he said, "or drink something, or sit down. She thinks I'm an old man."

Brick looked up at Claude; his face was sunburned, his hat pushed back. Brick reached out to touch his arm.

"Claude? Where are you?"

Claude winked at him. "I'm coming now," he shouted. "Have patience."

"I'm going to my house," Brick said. "I just want to see the trees . . ."

". . . from your porch," Claude finished for him.

Brick climbed over the fence then and turned back.

"Claude?" he called. "I'm going to learn French so I can read your book. And I'm going to read at school, study. I'm going to learn everything for this orchard." No more looking out the window in school, he thought. No more dreaming. *His orchard.*

Claude nodded. "Your mother will be happy."

"And Pop. Just wait till he hears, Claude."

Claude stood there for a moment, smiling. "I know," he said. "I know."

31

Mariel

Mariel had gone for a walk the next morning, trying to remember something. Something someone had said. Who? It wasn't one of the pickers; none of them had known her mother. They had just heard stories. At lunchtime, she went up the back steps to the kitchen, still thinking. It must have been something Joseph had said.

Claude and Brick were at the table, the radio blaring the game from the windowsill. In front of them was a crumpled little leaf and a book with pictures of trees and flowers.

When he saw her, Claude picked up a knife and a chunk of cheese. He sliced off a wedge for her, pushed a bottle of root beer closer, and stuck the tip of the knife into an apple. "Apples and cheese," he said. "There's nothing better in the world."

"Is that any way to give the child lunch?" Julia scolded, raising her hands and shaking her head at Mariel. "Deafening," she said. "Everything in the house vibrates because of that radio."

"Can you hear the noise of the crowd?" Claude asked, ignoring Julia. "Reiser just made a home run."

Julia rolled her eyes.

"Loretta took me to my first game," Mariel said. "It was a night game. It was early in the season, and very cold. I was afraid of the noise. Loretta wrapped her sweater around me." She could still feel the warmth of it, the feel of Loretta's hug.

Brick stopped flipping through the book. "Found it." He grinned. "A little dogwood tree, that's what it is. From Prospect Park."

Mariel leaned forward to run her finger over the leaf, thinking of the band shell, and Ambrose, and the fountain spraying water into the warm air.

Claude clapped his hand to his head. "I forgot about your letter," he said. "How could I do that?" He pulled it out of his pocket and slid it across the table to her.

She reached for it, so happy to see the envelope from Loretta. Loretta was writing every day. But when she picked it up, the writing wasn't Loretta's writing. The letters were large and even.

"It's not from Brooklyn," Claude said, shouting over the radio. "Queens, is it?"

"I don't know anyone from Queens." She ran her finger over the purple stamp, then turned the envelope over, tearing open the flap with the return address. "I can't imagine . . . ," she told them, looking down at the short note, the signature: *Vincent.*

She didn't know anyone named Vincent. Not in Brooklyn, not in Queens, not anywhere. She leaned over and read aloud: *"Dear Mariel, I miss walking with you in Brooklyn. Sometimes I walk with Loretta to her hospital. We talk about you and wonder what you're doing."*

She shook her head. No one walked with her in Brooklyn. And Loretta? Mariel could see her, always late, rushing down the street, no time to walk with anyone.

"Say hello to Billy Nightingale."

Ambrose? Could it be Ambrose the cop?

"Please come home, Mariel. It would make Loretta happy.

"Vincent."

Ambrose had a first name. Ambrose with the blue eyes, and the hat pushed back. She ran her hand over the paper. She missed Ambrose the cop, missed hiding on him, missed the shiny black shoes as he walked her to school. She turned the letter over. There was one last sentence. *"Loretta says to tell you I can cook."*

She smiled. If he could see their kitchen, the burned pots, she thought, and then something else. *If we ever get a husband in here . . .* Oh! She reached for a wedge of cheese, another apple. Loretta and *Ambrose?* Oh, how lovely.

"Mariel likes all this," Claude said. "Maybe we'll make a country girl out of her."

She looked up at him. His head was turned to one side. "A country girl?" she asked.

He watched her almost as if he were waiting for something.

And then she heard the voice of Red Barber, the announcer. "A grand slam," he said in a soft Southern drawl. But there was nothing soft about the noise of the crowd and Hilda the fan's cowbell clanging and clanging.

It was there, almost there, the thing she'd been trying to remember. Was it something to do with the radio? The Dodgers game? Loretta wrapping her in her sweater, hugging her?

She never even got to the hospital, Joseph had said.

Her hands were in front of her on the table, quiet now, no fluttering. But her heart was fluttering so hard she had to open her mouth to breathe. She closed her eyes.

She could see it in her mind: the middle of the night, a black square of window, the whoosh of the machine, all alone. And then her mother, the red sweater thrown over her shoulder, the charm bracelet dangling from one arm, clinking a little.

Her mother had never gotten to the hospital.

She leaned forward. Julia turned, her mouth open, ready to say something, but Claude warned her away with one large hand.

"You're going to get out of this iron lung, out of this hospital, I promise you. And then I'm going to take you home. I'll be your mother if you'll have me." She had bent over, so close that Mariel could smell the starch in her cap as it tumbled off her head.

Loretta, a red sweater over her white uniform. Loretta wearing a bracelet.

Loretta all the time.

"I'll be your mother. Won't I do? My child has had such a hard time, Mrs. Ginty. Here, look, knit one, purl one. You can do anything, Mariel. I'd come but you have to do this by yourself. President Roosevelt said, 'The only thing we have to fear is fear itself.' I love you, Mariel."

"Please." Mariel pushed herself away from the table. "I have to go home now."

32

Mariel

*I*t was a daytime bus, so Mariel could see the farms as they flashed by, and then the small towns turning into larger ones, with lovely gray stone buildings and houses with neat little gardens. Once they passed a redbrick school with a flag flying in front and kids playing jump rope in the yard.

She couldn't play jump rope. She thought about it, leaning against the window. Loretta would say she could, but she didn't have to jump rope; she didn't have to do everything.

They had hugged her at the Windy Hill bus station, all of them telling her she had to come back next summer. Julia had tears in her eyes as Claude put his hands on her shoulders. "We will never forget you,

Mariel," he said. "You were a brave girl to bring Brick home."

"And to bring the pickers," said Julia.

Mariel had reached up to ease the too-tight elastic of the hatband under her chin. "Will you write to me?" she asked Brick.

He nodded. He took one of her hands then, and hugged her at the same time. Then they stepped back, laughing, a little embarrassed.

"I don't think my fingers will flutter anymore," she said.

He raised one shoulder. "Even if they do it doesn't make any difference." He broke off. "I never had a friend like you."

"Oh, Billy Nightingale," she had said. "Me too."

She thought about it now in the bus. Why had it been so easy to be friends with Brick, and not with Geraldine Ginty?

After a while, they pulled into the Hurley bus station for a rest, and she bent over the water fountain for a cool drink. In back of her someone whispered. She put her head up in time to hear the end. "Poor kid . . . polio."

She smiled, the water from the fountain icy against her teeth, remembering the movie she and Loretta had seen, Dumbo the elephant with his large ears. *"And didn't he do just fine?" Loretta had said.*

Loretta had been talking about her.

From the other side of the station someone yelled, "Hey, the Dodgers just beat Cincinnati. They're hanging signs out in Brooklyn. They're going to win the pennant this time!"

A picture of Geraldine Ginty came into her mind. What would Geraldine say now about the Dodgers?

Mariel climbed back on the bus, thinking about Brooklyn, and Loretta, and Geraldine. She took a breath. Geraldine Ginty was afraid.

Could that be? Afraid of getting polio? Afraid of being like Mariel, hiding behind the stoop instead of playing? Fingers fluttering? Taking the backseat in school? *Razy Cray?*

Mariel pressed her nose against the window, seeing the darkness coming and lights going on here and there. But maybe it would be different now that Geraldine knew she had gone all the way upstate and back by herself.

She took a deep breath. She'd never hide behind the stoop again. She was going to start over. Geraldine might make an all-right friend, and so would Frankie McHugh. She'd make sure they really knew about President Roosevelt. And she'd show them she could hit, that maybe she was even a two-sewer hitter.

When the bus turned into the station in Manhattan, it was close to nine o'clock. Loretta stood there, her shiny black hair lifting as the bus slid in next to her.

Mariel sat there for just a moment. Loretta was standing up on tiptoes trying to see into the bus. Mariel could picture her in her starched white uniform, the pointy little cap, the red sweater over her shoulders, and the gold bracelet jingling, her face close to hers. How could she not have known it was Loretta coming back after her shift, spending all that time with her?

She reached up on the shelf over her head for the bag filled with apples, green leaves still clinging to the stems. *A green lace curtain. When the wind blows . . . knotted shoelaces, sweet face, a blue kerchief.*

My poor mother, she thought. She was hit with such a terrible sadness that for a moment she sat back in the seat again. *My mother.* Then she thought of Joseph: *The most important thing, she loved you.*

She took her purse and her hat off the seat next to her and looped them over her arm. She went along the aisle and climbed down the steps, dropping everything, her arms out to Loretta. They rocked back and forth, crying, laughing and talking both at once.

"I had to let you go."

"The two-dollar bill is gone, I'm sorry."

"We'll find another to remind us."

"I'll never leave again except for visits."

"Oh, honey."

"Oh, Loretta."

And then, at last, they turned to look at Ambrose the cop, who was gathering up the apples that rolled around their feet.

The Brooklyn Dodgers

It was September twenty-fifth. That afternoon the Dodgers were in Boston. It was the game that would matter, the one that would decide the pennant at last. In Brooklyn, radios blared from every house. Mrs. Warnicki had brought her own radio and put it on a table so the class could listen. And in Windy Hill, the principal promised to announce the score over the loud-speaker.

"Just get me one run," the pitcher Whitlow Wyatt told the rest of the team. "That's all I'm going to need." He told them he'd pitch the best game of his life. If it was the last thing he did, he'd never let one of the Braves get on base, much less hit a home run.

With every fan in Brooklyn glued to WOR and Red

Barber's soft voice describing all of it, the Dodgers got Wyatt his run in the first inning, and then another in the second, and one in the third. Reiser made sure he hit one in the seventh. And not one of the Braves was able to score.

The game ended at six to nothing. They'd won their first pennant in twenty years.

In Windy Hill, the noise in Brick's classroom was deafening. Brick closed his eyes, thinking of Reiser hitting that one in the seventh. He could almost see the ball with its red stitching spiraling through the air . . . but it wasn't this game, it was the one with the girl reaching up as the ball dropped, reaching and holding, and becoming his best friend.

A few minutes later, the principal of the Windy Hill school backed a truck filled with watermelons into the yard and the teachers cut slices for everyone, and the kids gathered around Brick, who was the only one of them who had ever been to Ebbets Field.

Brooklyn went wild. "We're in," people yelled from one window to another. Kids banged on dishpans, Fourth of July horns blared, and Mrs. Warnicki gave the class a night off with no homework, which was just as well. Everyone who could would be going to Grand Central Station to welcome the Dodgers as they came in on the 10:25 P.M. train from Boston.

Mariel was there wearing her straw hat, her blue party dress, and the old gold charm bracelet that Loretta had found for her. Loretta and Ambrose the cop were with her. They ate hot dogs from the vendor, drank root beer, and saw it all: Leo Durocher, the manager, stepping off the train onto the platform, Dixie Walker and Cookie Lavagetto waving, Hilda the fan clanging her cowbell.

"It was a good year," said Ambrose the cop. He reached for Mariel's hand, and then Loretta's.

"The best," said Mariel.

Pete Reiser heard them as he went by. "You can say that again," he said, tipping his hat, and he signed his name on their napkins.

·